SHE WAS THE FIRST . . .

Her legs worked furiously in a useless effort to outrace the black machine. Then she felt the touch of its hot body against her bare skin—a savage caress that telegraphed the end of her young life. The next instant her flesh was tearing as she was scraped along between the car and the guardrail . . . as her eyes swept past the windshield her dying brain recorded the sensory input of what she saw. It was only a brief glimpse through the murky depths of the amber glass, but . . . her last recollection was one of unspeakable horror at the presence that had glared back at her.

THE CAR

A Novel of Total, Shrieking Terror!

UNIVERSAL—AN MCA COMPANY

THE CAR

Starring

JAMES BROLIN

KATHLEEN LLOYD

JOHN MARLEY   R. G. ARMSTRONG

JOHN RUBINSTEIN

and **RONNIE COX** as Luke

Screenplay by
Dennis Shryack, Michael Butler, and Lane Slate

Story by
Dennis Shryack and Michael Butler

Produced by
Marvin Birdt and Elliot Silverstein

Directed by
Elliot Silverstein

THE CAR

A novel by
Dennis Shryack
and
Michael Butler

Based on a screenplay by
**Dennis Shryack, Michael Butler,
and Lane Slate**

A DELL BOOK

Published by
DELL PUBLISHING CO., INC.
1 Dag Hammarskjold Plaza
New York, New York 10017

Story by Dennis Shryack and Michael Butler.
Screenplay by Dennis Shryack, Michael Butler, and Lane Slate.

ISBN: 0-440-11032-7

Printed in the United States of America
First printing—May 1977

The tentative first light of dawn pierced the darkness. The air was still, awaiting the breath of a new day. Jagged, thrusting peaks began to materialize in a shadow play of subtle definition, stillborn sentinels keeping a blind watch on the slowly blanching night.

Far below, nestled in the solitude of peaceful, dreamless sleep, a young man and woman lay side by side, each wrapped in the warm confines of a colorfully quilted sleeping bag.

Pete, by nature an early riser, was the first to wake. He lay there, still in awe of the beauty that surrounded him even though he'd spent the whole of his nineteen years in its midst; then he turned to his companion and brushed her cheek lightly with a kiss.

Suzie stirred gently and he kissed her again. Her brown eyes opened, staring at him through the hazy recognition of half-sleep, and then a contented smile spread across her pretty face.

"Good morning," she said through a yawn.

"Good morning yourself. Sleep good?"

"Terrific. How about you?"

"The best," he answered. "There's nothing quite like it, is there?"

"Oh, I don't know," she said coyly. "A bed does have certain advantages."

"Really? I thought we did pretty good without one last night."

"Only pretty good? Well, thank you very much." She unzipped her bag and sat up, running her fingers through her flaxen hair.

"Hey, you know what I meant."

"Do I?"

"Will you stop that and give me a kiss?"

She couldn't suppress a teasing laugh as she shifted quickly out of his reach and stood up.

"If you'll excuse me, Mr. Tactful, I think it's my turn to fix breakfast."

"To hell with breakfast," he said as he struggled out of his bag and lunged for her.

She jumped away and ran through the damp meadow grass, laughing as he chased her.

Their joy was a natural counterpoint to the freshness of the morning, and as he caught up with her, the two of them tumbling to the earth in a twining of tanned, healthy young bodies, she offered only a token flurry of resistance before submitting to the passion that overwhelmed them both.

Hands fighting against buttons and zippers, their clothing was discarded in small explosions of khaki and plaid and soon they were naked in each other's arms, lost in their mutual pleasure.

Afterward, as they lay spent on the dew-covered grass, he propped himself up on an elbow and lazily traced the outline of her mouth with his finger.

"I wish this weren't the end," he said. "It's been a beautiful five days."

Suzie kissed his finger. "There'll be others: all the time in the world."

He grinned. "That's easy for you to say. Do you have any idea of what I had to go through to get away for this? My mother isn't exactly the most liberal person in the world, you know."

"It was worth it, wasn't it?"

He kissed her hard on the mouth.

"Suzie, can I say something crazy?"

"I wish you would," she whispered.

"I think I love you. I mean really love you."

She reached up and pulled him against her, surprised to find him ready so quickly. Then she felt him sliding in.

"Please," she said softly. "Let's make it slow this time." And they did, lavishing each other with new sensations as if, for some inexplicable reason, this would be their last time together.

Sunrise was perhaps an hour old, and the stoic grandeur of rugged mountains and swelling foothills dwarfed Pete and Suzie as they cycled along a narrow asphalt highway, its center line long ago faded to a ghostly streak.

They rode side by side, bright yellow backpacks secured, their young bodies poised effortlessly on their sleek ten-speed bikes. Their firm, well-muscled legs moved in an easy rhythm. They'd been riding only a few minutes, remarking casually on the passing scenery, tranquil and content in the leisurely pace of their journey.

An incline loomed in front of them, climbing to the top of a rock-studded cliff.

"Race you to the top!" Pete suddenly called across.

"You're on!" She flashed him a challenging smile, shifted gears, and jumped into a quick lead, the muscles tensing in the backs of her shapely thighs and straining against her snug-fitting white shorts.

Pete's response was pure reflex, a smooth performance of bike and rider as the drive chain slipped cleanly from one sprocket to another and he brought his body almost parallel to the asphalt in an attempt to minimize any wind drag.

As the hill grew steeper, beads of perspiration sprang out across their foreheads, but a simple change of gears kept their bikes going faster and faster. The road dropped off sharply to their right in a rocky cascade to the diminishing landscape below. With a quick glance over her shoulder, Suzie saw Pete determinedly closing the gap between them, but their competition was overlaid by a strong sense of joy, and neither could contain their laughter as their eyes met.

"You'll never make it!" he yelled.

"Says who?" She pumped faster, the cool morning air whipping past her face, the wind of her momentum lifting her hair from her shoulders.

Pete marveled at her body, taut and uncompromising in her effort to win, and thought back to the dawn, when she'd lain next to him, soft and supple after their bouts of lovemaking. He had a brief urge to let up, but he knew she'd be hurt at the concession, and he had to admit that there was a good chance he was going to lose no matter what he did. More than once during the past week she'd proven herself to be an excellent competitor; yet somehow she always managed to retain her femininity. He liked that immensely, her combination of beauty and strength. She was bright and athletic, and she wasn't ashamed of being either. She accepted a challenge on its own terms and asked for no special favors. She was eager to please, but demanded pleasure in return. In short, she was one hell of a woman, and the knowledge that they belonged to each other—not by acquisition but by freedom of choice—filled him with pride.

Nearing the crest of the hill, a good two hundred feet above the spot where they'd begun their climb, they each threw their bikes into the highest gear and bore down for the final big push to the top.

Their breathing was labored, their bodies tense with the challenge at hand. Pete's front wheel pulled up even with Suzie's legs, and then, in a final burst of speed, he crested the top of the hill and let out a joyful victory yell, Suzie pulling up beside him.

"How the hell did you do that?"

"Talent," he gloated. "Pure talent."

"And a lot of luck."

"Jealous?"

"Never!"

The top of the hill was fairly level for twenty-five or thirty yards, and they came to a stop at the entrance to a mile-long tunnel to catch their breath.

As they stood there, straddling their bikes and staring into the rock-hewn tube of darkness that stretched before them, they could read on each other's faces the identical thought: when they came out at the other end of that tunnel, it would be an easy, downhill ride into Santa Ynez—and the end of their idyllic trip.

A sudden gust of wind flurried, kicking up some dust, and Suzie broke the oppressive silence. "Hey! Race you through the tunnel!"

"Haven't had enough, huh?"

Just as the two of them lurched into the blackness of the tunnel, the faint rumble of an engine nudged the early-morning languor. But the impression barely registered with them; there was a race to be won, and that was all that commanded their attention.

A mile and a half away, a car moved along the same road, its black bulk digesting the asphalt in a frenzy of forward progress. Riding the center line, it snaked quickly around hairpin turns with uncanny agility, as if it were alien to no road on earth. As it rose into the mountains, the roar of its engine lacerated the post-dawn stillness.

Inside the car vacant silence reigned, underlined only by the smooth hum of a massive power plant. Otherwise, not the slightest sound could be heard as the scenery rushed by like a silent film unreeling past amber, smoke-tinted windows.

The dashboard of the car was devoid of all standard Detroit paraphernalia, with the exception of a thin red needle monitoring the pace of the machine on a horizontal slash of speedometer. The windshield, tinted amber like all the other glass, offered an eerie perspective of the fast-approaching world.

Within the tunnel, the two cyclists hurtled onward, the light at the other end growing steadily brighter, the arching ribs of the supporting structure vaulting high above their heads.

The hill that had tested the skills and endurance of Pete and Suzie vanished beneath the wheels of the car like so much meat passing into a grinder. In less than a minute it had topped the grade, its huge mass taking briefly to the air, then settling down again with the grace of a big cat.

Pete and Suzie shot out of the tunnel, racing downhill. To their right ran a stone guardrail; beyond that, the road dropped off sharply into a deep chasm. On their left, giant red cliffs rose up into the clean morning air.

The car entered the tunnel, single headlamps popping on, the spill of the illumination glancing off the highly polished maw of its vertical grill.

Like a capsule whisking through a pneumatic tube, the car hissed through the long rock passageway, the throb of its engine a steadily rising crescendo that trumpeted out toward the cyclists.

As it broke into the sunlight, they glanced nervously over their shoulders at the scream of the approaching car, still rendered invisible by the S-curves that lay behind them. They'd both done enough riding to be more than familiar with road jocks, and they edged a little closer to the stone guardrail, still pumping hard and waiting for the inevitable moment when the car would pass, probably with its horn blaring or the idiot driver shouting some obscenity.

Suzie, about five yards behind Pete, was the first to detect a change in the engine's pitch as the car slowed dramatically. She looked back just in time to see it slide into view around a tight curve. Shocked at its menacing presence, she watched it leave its position over the center line and pull in directly behind the two of them.

Damn, she thought, *he wants to play games. Just what we need.*

More than a little apprehensive, she waved the car around with her left arm.

Its response was to increase its speed and pull up to within twenty feet of her.

Pete looked back. "What the hell is he trying to do? Come on around!" he yelled, and he waved the car by.

It closed the gap to within ten feet of Suzie. Frightened, she shifted gears and bore down hard on the pedals of her bike.

Again the car accelerated, halving the distance between them. Pete saw what was happening, but there was nothing either of them could do. To their right was the guardrail and the drop of the cliff; to their left, the mountainside; and behind them, the car.

The palms of Suzie's hands began to sweat and slip

along the black tape on her handlebars. Her mouth went dry with fear. She was traveling as fast as she could, and still the car dogged her from five feet away, the heat of its engine beating against her bare legs.

Why doesn't he pass? Why doesn't he pass? The litany ran through her mind over and over again. Then, abruptly, the car moved to its left.

Thank God, she thought.

She felt its presence as it pulled alongside her rear wheel, and forced herself not to turn and look, afraid that any reaction on her part might prompt the driver to some new game of madness. Gradually her peripheral vision picked up the sparkling chrome of a double bumper and the hump of a rounded, inwardly-canted front fender that jutted out beyond the headlight like the bulbous shoulder of a circus strongman.

Move, damn you! Move! The unspoken words rang loud and clear in her head. Skillfully, she maneuvered her rocketing bike even closer to the stone guardrail in an attempt to give the car as wide a berth as possible. Then, somehow, she sensed it was going to make another move, and for a moment she felt relief, but it was quickly shattered by the realization of what was about to happen.

"PETER!" The name was wrenched from her throat in a shriek of fear.

He turned, disbelief mingling with terror as he watched the car creep to its *right,* forcing Suzie over; now she was only inches from the railing.

Her legs worked furiously in a useless effort to outrace the black machine. Then she felt the touch of its hot body against her bare skin—a savage caress that telegraphed the end of her young life. The next instant her flesh was tearing as she was scraped along between the car and the guardrail, her bicycle ripped in two by the grinding friction. She screamed once, a tortured plea for help, and Pete couldn't bring himself to turn and witness what he knew was happening.

Seconds later, Suzie's body was spun completely around by the action of the car. As her eyes swept past the windshield, her dying brain recorded what she saw. It was only a brief glimpse through the murky depths of the amber glass, but it was a glimpse at close range, and her last recollection was one of unspeakable horror at the presence that had glared back at her, burning its image into her clouding mind. Then her mangled corpse and the twisted remains of part of her bike plunged over the side, the railing having terminated a few feet before the beginning of a bridge.

Pete leaned into his bike's momentum, his mind a paralyzed mass, frozen on the tableau of his impending death.

The car drew up behind his rear wheel, the noise of the engine beating a furious tattoo in his ears. He felt the slightest impact as its bumper gently nudged his bike. He couldn't help it, he was ashamed, but tears rolled down his face. He just wanted it to be over.

The car backed off slightly, then again contacted the rear of Pete's bike. His knuckles blanched white with the grip of his hands on the bars. He'd never considered his own death before, most certainly not in violent terms, and now it was upon him. In one quick, savage movement, the car leapt forward with coiled fury, its front bumper literally scooping up Pete and his fragile bike and flinging them off the bridge and into the chasm below. Pete's dying scream was lost on the rugged wilderness.

The car hurtled on as if nothing had happened, leaving behind it three signposts of death: a ghastly crimson streak staining a section of the railing, a twisted portion of a bicycle, and a tattered piece of a plaid blouse.

The evidence was there, waiting to be discovered, waiting for the fear to begin.

The sharp rays of the morning sun filtered through a thin pair of abstract-printed curtains and laid down a bright splash of light across the sleeping figure of Wade Parent, Jr.

Turning restlessly, he buried his face in the pillow; but it was useless, and soon his eyes struggled open in grudging acceptance of a new day.

He stretched luxuriously in the double bed and then, as his thoughts settled into place, he realized that the other half of the bed was empty. A wry smile crossed his face as he turned over, propped himself up on an elbow, and looked across the room, knowing exactly what he'd find.

Lauren, draped in Wade's beige terry bathrobe, sat passively in the lotus position, her back to the bed and her head tilted up to receive the full morning light that streamed through the window.

"Jesus," he muttered under his breath. An uncomplicated man, Wade simply couldn't understand Lauren's attachment to yoga, something he regarded as nothing more than a childish diversion. He'd tried to talk her out of it months ago, but she'd only smiled and told him he didn't know what he was missing. The second time he'd brought it up the conversation had taken a spiritual bent, and that had made him uncomfortable.

Certainly he believed in a supreme force, but it was a vague, highly personalized conception. And even though Wade's mother had been a devout Methodist, extremely active in the church functions of the little town of Santa Ynez, it made little difference to Wade whether people referred to their God as Christ, Jehovah, or something else. To him, a person's life was largely of his own making. As a police officer and a police officer's son, he'd seen too many decent people fall on hard times and too many bastards muddle through untouched to believe that there was anything even close to a divine plan. And if there were, then it sure as hell must have been scrapped a very long time ago.

People, he reasoned, were here to do the best they could, and that was that.

The alarm went off, its shrill message annoying Wade. Lauren, he noticed, didn't so much as flinch at the sudden intrusion. He slapped down the button on the top of the clock, killing the sound. Throwing back the covers, he got out of bed, his tall, lean frame clothed only in rumpled white shorts. He brushed a shock of dark hair from his forehead and walked across the room.

Standing behind Lauren, he bent down and kissed the top of her head, then began to massage her shoulders gently with his strong hands. She made no response and he stopped, exasperated.

"Aren't you ever going to give up on this thing?"

Her body still remained motionless. Then he slipped the robe from her back and slid his hands across her full, bare breasts, keeping it up until the nipples became erect beneath his palms.

Leaning back against his legs, she opened her eyes and looked up at him, her softly sensuous features framed by her dark brown hair.

"You're interrupting my meditation," she said.

"You're damn right I am."

He lifted her to her feet, the robe remaining in a heap on the floor. Turning her around, he kissed her, running his fingertips gently along her spine and across the swell of her buttocks.

"Know what?" she asked.

"What?"

"This sure beats the hell out of sitting on the floor."

Smiling, he led her to the bed.

Bertha Clements lay in bed, listening to the steady rise and fall of her husband's breathing, feeling the anger and humiliation rise within her as it had done so many times in the past. He treated her like chattel. She knew that, and the knowledge told her she was just as much to blame for her predicament as Amos was.

How many times had she resolved to do something about their farce of a marriage, and how many times had the resolve evaporated in the face of his drunken curses and taunting challenges? There had been a time when she'd had herself convinced that she could handle the situation, that she could give him a certain amount of slack and still make it clear that she had her boundaries of pride that must not be crossed. But those boundaries had gradually widened until they'd ceased to have any meaning, and little by little she'd been reduced to the level of a spectator watching her own existence. Her life was in motion before her eyes and she was completely powerless to do anything about it. Indignity had been piled upon indignity until she found it difficult to remember what it meant to be treated with respect.

She'd let it all be done to her, because almost twelve years ago, when she'd felt love for someone else and had been afraid to express it, Amos had come along— brash and forceful—and made everything easy for her, offering her an escape from her self-imposed problems, a welcome relief from the burden of decision.

At first she'd envied his lack of inhibitions, his all-stops-out attack on life; then she'd gradually come to realize that it was all a charade and that he existed behind a mask just as much as she did, but by then it had been too late.

This morning, waiting for him to waken from his alcoholic dreams, her sense of shame gnawing at her with growing intensity, she resolved that somehow, some way, she had to reclaim at least a modicum of her self-respect.

Then, in the midst of a mental preview of the ugly scene she knew was sure to take place when she had it out with him, the jarring sound of someone playing a horn invaded the quiet of their cramped bedroom.

"Shit," Amos said, squinting through bloodshot eyes, "what the hell's going on?"

"Forget about it; I want to talk to you." She stared at the ceiling, afraid to face him.

Ignoring her, he looked at the alarm clock. "God-damnit! I coulda slept for another half hour." He jammed his bare feet into a pair of scuffed slippers and headed for the closet to get his robe.

Bertha sat on the edge of the bed. "I said I wanted to talk to you."

She flinched as he whirled around.

"About what?" he snapped.

"About last night." The words came out almost as a plea.

"My life is my own, Bertha. Understand?"

Outside, the notes from the horn continued to fill the air, resolving themselves into a glib, frolicsome tune that lent a tragicomic counterpoint to the argument in the bedroom.

"Your life involves me, Amos. And our son."

"Leave the boy out of it."

"How can I? You think he doesn't know what's going on? You think I don't know? What am I supposed to do? Sit back and smile while you spend the night with some bar woman?"

"Shut up! Just shut up! I'll do as I damn well please, and if you don't like it you can leave any time you want."

Their exchange carried clearly from within the small house; it was followed immediately by the sharp sound of a slap and a woman's cry.

"Amos, you do that again and I'll call the police! I mean it!"

Again the sound of a slap cracked through the air, and Bertha came dashing out of the house, across the porch, and down the steps. Amos chased after her, his thin wiry body moving with vengeful speed. It was only the incongruous sight of a young man sitting across the road, French horn in hand, that brought them both to a momentary stop.

The young man, his back resting against a road sign that announced the Santa Ynez city limits, got slowly to his feet and surveyed the unlikely couple across the dusty highway. The woman, it was easy to see, had once been attractive, though now her figure was on the plump side.

"Everything okay over there?" the young man asked cautiously.

"None of your goddamn business!" Amos yelled. Then he wheeled on his wife, who was obviously embarrassed by their unexpected audience. "I'm gonna come home at night when I'm good and damn ready, and I don't want any crap from you! You got me?"

"Amos, please, let's go back inside." Her voice was hollow and hesitant.

Amos raised a threatening hand.

"Hey, mister!"

The young man drew a vicious glare from Amos.

"You want part of this, just come on across the street. I owe you one anyway for waking me up with that fucking bugle."

"Couldn't have been me. This is a French horn, not a bugle."

"I don't give a shit what it is. And don't try to get smart with me, or I'll shove that horn up your ass!"

"Just keep it cool, man. Keep it cool. I'm putting it away. See?"

He bent down and laid the instrument in its case. "You see how nicely it fits and how silent it is?"

"What the hell are you sayin' now?"

"Seems to me *you're* doing most of the talking, sir."

"Then hear this: I'm givin' you five minutes to move your ass out of here."

"I'll be glad to oblige you, soon as my thumb gets a little action."

Amos muttered something indistinguishable, then turned and walked back into the house. His wife stood awkwardly in the shabby, rock-infested front yard, wishing she had the nerve to apologize for her husband's behavior.

The young man felt sorry for her. "No harm done," he called across. "You sure you're okay?"

She was about to thank him for his kindness when Jimmy, her ten-year-old son, opened the front door and leaned out, rubbing the sleep from his eyes.

"Pa says for you to come and get breakfast started. He's hungry."

She gave one last glance at the hitchhiker, then obediently went inside and shut the door behind her.

The young man stood there, shaking his head at what he'd just seen, when he noticed the lettering on a truck parked several yards from the house:

AMOS CLEMENTS
Granite, Gravel & Blasting

He chuckled to himself. Old Amos certainly had a disposition to match his profession.

Determined not to let the incident spoil his day, the hitchhiker prepared himself for travel. Positioning himself beneath the black-and-white road sign, he looked expectantly down the meager excuse for a highway.

After a few minutes of staring into a singularly uninspiring stretch of landscape, he thought he saw something in the far, far distance. Smoothing his hair with his hand, tugging the wrinkles out of his lightweight safari jacket, he lofted his thumb jauntily into the air.

Psyching himself up to a positive attitude, he began to fantasize about the approaching ride—a little routine he often used to bring himself luck.

This is it, he told himself; *he's gonna stop. Actually, she's gonna stop. And she's gonna be, oh, a thirty-four-year-old nympho in short-shorts and a skin-tight T-shirt, with a definite aversion to underwear.*

She'll skid to a stop in her two-seater Jag.

Hi, I'll say, my name's John Norris. What's yours? My, but you're a darlin'-looking lady. I'll pay the tolls and we'll have ourselves some good times.

Then she'll swing her gorgeous body into the other seat so I can drive, and we're off to . . . the Amazon Basin to water-ski.

I'm ready. Yessir, I think I can handle it.

He continued to stare at the approaching object—which, due to the angle of the sun, looked like mirrors dancing down the highway toward him. Strangely enough, he couldn't make up his mind whether the illusion was eerie or cheerful. But in any case, it was a potential ride.

The closer it got, the more aware he became of its speed.

"Come on, darlin', you keep that up and you're not even going to see me."

The first whine of its engine reached his ears, and a car began to take shape in the glinting sunlight—a black, hulking mass hurtling forward at a menacing pace.

Suddenly, out of the still morning air, a flurry of wind swirled around him, throwing dust from the soft shoulder of the road into his eyes. He wiped his face clear with his left hand, keeping his right thumb staunchly in the air.

From only fifty yards away, the car was an ominous sight, and John found himself backing up, inching closer to the Santa Ynez signpost. Then, in a savagely graceful movement, the car veered to its right, the snout of its hood and its two gaping headlights bearing down on him like a crazed beast.

Immobilized by disbelief, he drew in his breath as the screaming machine shot past him, clearing his slender body by no more than a few life-saving inches.

The hot smell of its engine still in his nostrils, John whirled and thrust his middle finger high into the air in a furious salute.

"Up yours, you stupid sonofabitch!" he screamed after the fast-receding car.

Just as he let his hand drop to his side, he heard the screech of locked brakes, and the car fishtailed to a halt. It sat there for a moment, the engine pulsing steadily; then it began to slowly back up.

John's mouth was dry with anger. If the bastard wanted a fight, that was okay with him, even though he knew he'd probably come out on the short end. In any event, there wasn't a hell of a lot he could do about it, unless he wanted to take refuge in Amos Clements' house, and he'd rather suffer a beating than do that.

He was telling himself to go for the guy's vulnerable spots—a swift kick in the balls, a hard jab to his nose—when he realized that the car was picking up speed, the rear tires biting into the road for traction.

For perhaps two seconds he stood rooted to the spot as the car accelerated rapidly, his brain frantically trying to formulate the impulses that might save his life. But it was too late.

John screamed at the impact. The rear bumper shattered his kneecaps, and an instant later he was flying through the air, his body twisting uncontrollably. Then he was striking the pavement face down, the sound of his splintering jaw a curious crackle in his ears.

He lay there, wondering why he felt no pain, his mind a jumbled circuit of present and past, when he heard the car once again screech to a halt.

He managed to roll over on his back and then, when he saw what was happening, the cry that escaped from his twisted mouth was born of pure, undiluted fear.

The black machine rolled forward, its right front tire passing across John's legs at the thighs, bloody pieces of flesh and fragments of bone adhering to the tread.

His final scream brought Amos Clements rushing to his front door. He watched, dumbfounded, as the car rolled back and forth over its victim's body, methodically grinding it to a barely recognizable mass of dirt and pulp. Then it roared off down the highway as a thick cloud of dust settled over what remained of John Norris.

Amos gagged, his bile mixing with the taste of the coffee he'd just finished. Then his hand flew to his mouth and he raced for the kitchen sink.

Lauren stood beside Wade's bed, buttoning the front of a pale-blue long-sleeved dress. Though it was simple and straightforward, the contours of her body made it look like something special. Wade, his hands clasped behind his head on a pillow and a sheet pulled up to his waist, couldn't take his eyes off her.

She smiled and glanced at a photograph on the wall. "Do you think your father would have approved?"

Wade looked across at the photo, the handsome, leathery face staring back at him from beneath a full head of snow-white hair.

"Approved? Hell, he probably would've fought me for you."

"And won?"

"I wouldn't want to make any bets, I'll tell you that. He was one fine man."

"I wish I could have known him."

"You would have liked him. He had a way of letting people know what he was all about just by shaking their hands and looking them in the eye. That's why he made such a damn good sheriff; people respected him. They knew he was a human being first and a cop second. And somehow, one never got in the way of the other."

"He must have had a great many friends."

"Damn near the whole town liked him, really *liked* him. When he died, an awful lot of people felt they'd lost a good friend. . . . Hell, I sound like a goddamn commercial. We'll both be late for work if I don't shut up." His words came out a little loud in a self-conscious effort to shrug off what he'd been saying.

"Shhh," Lauren said. "You'll wake your children."

"It's time they got up anyway."

"Not while I'm here, it isn't."

"Come on, you know they're wild about you."

"Wild about me is one thing; finding me in their father's bedroom is quite another."

"They've got to learn sooner or later."

"Look who's talking? If they walked in here right now you'd be the first one to jump for cover, and you know it."

He smiled, knowing full well she was right. "Are you trying to tell me I'm going to have to make an honest woman out of you?"

"That, Deputy, is entirely up to you." She bent over and gave him a quick kiss. "Love you; shall I come over tonight and fix dinner for you and the kids?"

"We'll be waiting."

She walked across the room, picked up her purse from the maple dresser, and quietly left the room, closing the door behind her.

Wade lay there, turning their conversation over in his mind, and knowing that for all Lauren's patience and understanding, he'd have to make a move soon. They had a very comfortable relationship, but he could tell she wanted it to be more than that. She had too much pride to be strung along indefinitely. Hell, he thought, when you came right down to it, she was just too damn *smart* to put up with a life like that. And he couldn't blame her. No, the situation demanded action—had for several months—yet he was still trying to kid himself into believing that he could put it off.

He cursed his hesitation. Gutless, that's what his father would have called him, and he would have been right; because it wasn't that Wade didn't want to make a commitment to Lauren. The truth, quite simply, was that he was afraid. Afraid of another disaster like his first marriage. To this day, he couldn't begin to fathom the sudden and complete change that had come over his wife—ex-wife now, thank God.

Everything had been fine for those first few years. Then, once the house had a nice chunk of equity in it and he'd chalked up a little seniority with the department, they'd decided to start a family. Joyce had been ecstatic when she'd learned she was pregnant. They'd driven to the closest thing resembling a big town and celebrated with fancy food and champagne at even fancier prices.

When Lynn Marie had been born, much of their daily routine had been turned upside down. But neither of them had cared. During those first weeks of a newborn baby's constant hunger, they'd even taken turns with the legendary two o'clock feeding. In fact, Wade could still remember struggling out of bed, warming a bottle, and positioning himself in a corner of the sofa with his tiny new daughter in his arms.

As for his wife, she'd shown all the symptoms of being a perfect mother: worrying about whether the baby was gaining enough weight or getting enough sleep, constantly consulting all the pediatrics books she could get her hands on.

A year later, Debra had been born. Though that pregnancy had taken them both by surprise, they'd adjusted to it without any great difficulty. Or at least, that's what Wade had thought.

The years had passed uneventfully enough (maybe too much so, now that he looked back on them); the girls had grown and started elementary school; everything had seemed to be just as it should be.

Then, one day, he'd come home for lunch and found a note: Joyce had gone into the city to do some shopping. He hadn't thought anything of it until that evening, when he'd seen what she'd bought. There were cocktail dresses, negligees, expensive imported perfumes, almost a thousand dollars' worth of merchandise—an expenditure they certainly couldn't afford.

He'd tried to reason with her, but it had done no good —all it had accomplished was to start a bitter, ugly scene during which she'd lashed out at everything their life together had been. It had ended with Wade's being left to comfort their crying, frightened children.

The following day, he'd had no choice but to return the things she'd bought. As a peace offering, he'd suggested that she keep one of the more expensive negligees, and her response had been to toss it into the fireplace.

The ensuing months had been a private hell that still left him depressed and shaken when he thought about them. The girls had begun doing poorly in school; mealtimes had become tension-filled ordeals; he'd begun finding excuses to work extra shifts, and then had hated himself for leaving his daughters alone with her. . . .

Then, as suddenly as it had begun, it was over. He got a call one afternoon at the station from Lynn Marie —she and Debra had just gotten home from school.

"Mommy's gone, her clothes and everything."

That was all the little girl could bring herself to say, and Wade would never forget the hurt and bewilderment in her voice for the rest of his life.

A few days later, a letter arrived. Joyce wanted no part of Wade or their children. It was a simple statement, most cooperative in tone, and it assured him that when he filed for divorce, she would do nothing to stop him.

Once it was settled, he was surprised to discover that the sense of relief actually outweighed the reality of failure. And he could see it in his daughters, too. He marveled at their resiliency, and they went out of their way to make it clear that they didn't hold him responsible for their mother's actions.

That had all been a little over two years ago. The girls were ten and nine now; Lauren was in his life, and he loved her. Why the hell couldn't he bring himself to do anything about it?

Glancing at the clock on the nightstand, he saw that he was running late. He bounded out of bed, put on the fallen bathrobe Lauren had been wearing, and walked down the short hall to the children's room.

Opening the door, he immediately saw that they were pretending to be asleep. It was a game they often played, and, tiptoeing across the room, he made a quick lunge at the covers and ripped them off the beds to an immediate chorus of squeals and giggles of delight.

"All right, you two phonies, we're late, so let's shake a leg. It'll have to be cold cereal for breakfast this morning; think you can handle that, Debbie?"

"Oh, Daddy," she said in her most exasperated tone, "of course I can."

"Unless she drops the milk again," Lynn Marie chimed in.

"That was 'cause you bumped me, and you know it!"

"Hey," he interrupted, "I don't plan to starve to death in the meantime. Lynn, you fix the coffee while I'm shaving."

"And try to remember to plug it in this time," Debbie said smugly.

Wade threw up his hands in total helplessness and left the room.

Twenty-five minutes later, Debbie and Lynn Marie stood in the driveway of their modest brick home. They were dressed in blue jeans and colorful blouses, and each had a black-and-white crash helmet tucked under her arm.

Inside, Wade crossed from the house into a connecting, barnlike structure that doubled as a spacious workroom and garage. The paraphernalia scattered about reflected his love for engines, though between Lauren and the children he hadn't found much time lately to indulge his hobby.

Adjacent to the workroom was a shed that held Wade's large, powerful motorcycle. Wiping some dust from the seat and giving the chrome headlamp a couple of quick buffs with the shirt sleeve of his tan sheriff's uniform, he straddled the bike and walked it outside.

Though it was a daily ritual, the girls' eyes seldom failed to light up with excitement when they saw their father astride the shiny machine.

The engine kicked over with a deep, throaty rumble, and he waved them over. "Come on, let's go!"

Anxiously, they ran across the concrete drive and stuffed their books into the twin satchels over the rear wheel of the bike. Then, their helmets fastened, they climbed aboard behind Wade: Debbie wrapping her arms around his waist, Lynn Marie holding firmly onto her younger sister.

"Ready?"

"All set," they answered.

"Okay, then, here we go."

They pulled out into the street, moving along at a very moderate speed. They hadn't gone far when Lynn Marie self-consciously cleared her throat and spoke above the steady throb of the engine.

"Daddy?"

"Yeah?"

"When are you going to get married?"

"What!?" Wade shot a swift glance back at the two of them.

"When are you going to get married?" Lynn Marie repeated, trying very hard to keep from giggling.

"To Lauren," Debbie added, suddenly horrified at the thought that their father might have someone else in mind.

Wade chuckled and shook his head at their directness. "Don't you think you two are jumping the gun a little bit?"

"We think you love her," Lynn Marie said, and this time she did giggle—and drew a stern over-the-shoulder look from Debbie.

"Well?" Debbie prodded. "Don't you?"

A distant sound pricked a remote corner of Wade's mind, coming and going in the space of a blink.

"Come on, Daddy," Lynn said. "You told us once that if we ever had anything serious to talk to you about, to do it."

Wade debated his answer for a moment, then decided on the truth. "Okay, I love her."

"See," Debbie said to her sister, "I told you so."

"But," Wade said, "that doesn't automatically mean that we're going to get married."

"Why not?" the girls asked almost in unison.

He caught the sound again, struggling to identify it, but Lynn Marie's insistent voice broke his concentration.

"If you love her, why not?"

"It takes two people to get married, honey. What I'm saying is, it depends just as much on Lauren as it does on me."

"Then ask her," Debbie said.

The simplicity of her logic was almost embarrassing to Wade.

"Daddy." Lyn Marie chose her words carefully. "We like Lauren a lot, really we do, and we know it was bad with you and Mom, but it could be good this time, couldn't it?"

Wade reached behind, squeezed his elder daughter's arm, and smiled. Touched by their love and awareness, he drove along for a few moments without saying anything. Then suddenly the sound defined itself and the roar of a powerful engine colored the background of his thoughts. The noise grew in intensity with terrible swiftness, and he felt Debbie's arms tighten around his waist. Seconds later, it was upon them, looming ferociously in the rearview mirror. A violent rush of air whipped their bodies as a large diesel van sped past at a good seventy-five miles per hour.

Wade immediately switched on his transmitter, holding the compact mike in his right hand. "This is four-oh-two."

A pleasant-sounding female voice filtered back through the tiny speaker. "Good morning, Wade. What's up?"

"I've got the kids and I'm on my way in, but there's an over-anxious diesel rig running north on Carter, cracking seventy-five at least. A unit should be able to nail him over at Webster."

"Right, will do."

They pulled up in front of the school and the girls slid off the bike, retrieving their books from the satchels.

"So what about it, Daddy?" Debbie asked.

"You two don't give up, do you?"

"We just want you to be happy," Lynn Marie said. "That's all."

"And that's what I want for all three of us," he answered. "So the minute the time is right, I'll ask her."

A loud cheer went up from the two girls, causing some of the other children to look in their direction.

"Now listen," Wade said, "this is just between us; I mean that."

"We won't say anything."

"We promise."

"And don't get your hopes up too high; she can always turn me down, you know."

"No way!" They were a duet of unbridled confidence.

"Okay, okay. Now get in there where you belong."

They each gave him a quick kiss on the cheek and ran across the street to the school yard.

Wade watched them go, proud that they belonged to him, and more than a little chagrined that they saw so clearly what had to be done.

"Four-oh-two . . . four-oh-two . . . Wade, are you there?" Donna's voice crackled across his radio.

"Fire away, kid."

"There's a Code Four on Highway Nineteen—Amos Clements' house, about five miles out. Can you handle?"

"I'm on my way."

He made a U-turn in the street and was gone.

IV

As Wade pulled up to the scene, he could see that his was to be the last official arrival. The ambulance was already there, and so was Everett Peck, the sheriff, and Luke Johnson, another deputy. In fact, Wade began to wonder just why he'd been called in at all. There were certainly more than enough men there to handle a hit-and-run.

Leaning his heavy bike on its kickstand, he made his way around the ambulance. A passenger car approached, slowing to gawk, and Wade impatiently waved it by: he never could bring himself to understand the morbid curiosity that surrounded an accident. It was bad enough somebody had to get killed; why did the living have to take such a perverse interest in it?

Just then, one of the ambulance attendants walked up to him, shaking his head.

"Good morning, Wally."

"It sure as hell ain't. You better get a good hold on your breakfast before you go any farther."

"That bad, huh?"

"It's the most godawful mess *I've* ever seen," Wally said. "And believe me, I've had my share."

"Sorry."

"So am I; I'm the one who has to shovel him up."

Wally continued on to the ambulance. A few seconds later, Wade caught sight of the body.

"Jesus Christ," he said, turning his head away from the bloody pile of remains. He could feel the nausea churning in his stomach as he walked up to Everett and Luke, who were questioning Amos Clements.

"Morning, Wade," Everett said.

"Yeah. You sure know how to start a guy's day off right. What the hell hit him, a goddamn freight train?"

"Why don't you ask Amos?"

"I already told you once," Amos answered angrily.

"Good," Wade said. "Now tell us again."

"Why?"

"Because we got a mound of meat over there that used to be a walking, talking human being. And I want to know exactly what happened to him. So start your story; I'm all ears."

Wade listened as Amos recounted the incident with the young man and his horn.

"I'm surprised he didn't stick it in your ear, Amos."

"Listen, he was the one disturbing the peace! I had every right to be pissed off, and nobody can tell me different."

"Okay, okay. Then what happened?"

Amos lost his indignation and stared at the ground. "I heard a scream. I went to the door and . . ." he lifted his head and looked Wade in the eye. "That car didn't just hit him, it *attacked* him. Backward, forward, it just kept rolling over him till there was nothing left."

The brutality of the scene made Wade lose a beat in his questioning. Then he recovered. "Sounds like whoever did it wanted to make sure. How many times did you say the car hit him?"

"He knows as much as I do," Amos said, gesturing to Everett.

"But I'm asking *you*."

Amos spat on the ground and looked back at Wade. "Four times, I guess. Maybe five." His eyes were hard and his forehead wrinkled with anger.

"You told me four," Everett interrupted.

"What the hell difference does it make? Five times gonna make him any deader than four? You ought to be out trying to catch the bastard that did it instead of worrying about how many times the boy got run over."

Wade shot Everett a brief glance and got the almost indecipherable nod he was expecting in return.

"What kind of car was it, Amos?" Wade's voice had just the slightest edge to it.

"I don't know."

"Why don't you know?" Everett asked.

"You said you saw it," Wade cut in. "Was it foreign or domestic?"

"I'm no good at that kind of thing; it was just a car."

"Color?"

"I don't know . . . black, dark gray."

"Sedan?" Everett chopped the word off.

"What the hell, am I on trial here? A lot was going on, you know. A man was being killed; I didn't exactly expect to see that when I came to the door." He ran a hand through his thick, graying hair.

"Wagon? Hardtop? Convertible? Two-door? Four-door?" Wade rushed right in on top of Amos' excuse, forcing him to concentrate on the hitchhiker's death.

"I think it was a two-door."

"All right; landau top? Sunroof? Was it modified? Chopped, channeled?"

"Jesus! A guy was getting ground to hamburger; I wasn't taking notes!"

"What about the plates?" Wade continued. "What

about the color of the plates? Did you see any numbers?"

Amos looked to Everett for help. "What the hell does he want from me?"

"Did it have a *plate?*" Wade shouted.

"I don't know!"

"Shit, man, you're our only witness and you're telling us you don't know? Think! Six digits on our plates. Did it have six? Was it out-of-state?"

"I said I don't know!"

"You saw it!"

"I didn't see nothin'! How do you like that?"

"Bullshit! You saw two doors! And a murder!"

"With all that dust in the air, how could I tell anything for sure?"

"What do you mean, 'for sure'?" Wade prodded.

"I think . . . I don't think there were any plates, and the top was kind of squeezed down low. Now leave me alone, for Christ's sake! I've already been through more than any man should go through in one day!"

Everett looked at Wade, signaling enough.

"That'll do for now, Amos," Wade said.

"It damn well better do you for good. I ain't going through that again for nobody."

Everett gave him a benevolent smile, then walked away with Wade. Luke Johnson, the other deputy, who had stood silently by during the rapid-fire questioning, followed the two men toward the sheriff's car. A stocky man of medium height, Luke had a dominantly sensitive face, and as the ambulance attendants passed by with what was left of the young hitchhiker, Luke unconsciously fingered the gold crucifix that dangled from a chain around his neck.

When they reached the car, Everett opened the

passenger door and slumped sideways into the front seat. He was an altogether average, hard-working man who was conscientious about his work as sheriff. A veteran of the department, he had served under Wade's father for several years. But things were different now, even in a small town like Santa Ynez. For a long time he'd tried to tell himself that life was life, and things would essentially continue unchanged. But he'd never really believed it, and something like this only reinforced the nagging realization that people, and the things they were capable of doing to each other, were far different from what they'd used to be.

"Shit," Everett said wearily, "a two-door car—maybe black, maybe dark gray, with maybe no plates and a channeled top. What the hell kind of a description is that from someone who watched a guy being pulverized across the street from his own house?"

Wade could sense more than anger in Everett's question; there was helplessness there, too, and it made Wade uncomfortable. He felt a strong kinship with the sheriff, stretching back to the days when Wade's father had brought a then-young deputy by the name of Everett Peck home for an occasional Sunday dinner. Everett had always been a little stiff and self-conscious at the affairs, and undoubtedly there had been many Sundays when he'd had better things to do, but Wade Parent, Sr., had been a difficult, if not impossible, man to turn down, especially when you worked for him—or happened to be his only son.

"Anybody got any ideas on this thing?" Everett asked. "Because I'm sure open to suggestions."

"Just the obvious," Luke answered. "That whoever was driving the car *wanted* to wipe that kid out. Like Amos said, the guy was attacked. Which means we better look into his background real close and see if we can come up with some enemies."

Everett sighed at the magnitude of the situation. "That boy could be from anywhere, even Canada. In the meantime, the only thing I can do is get on the horn, call Daigler County in case the car crossed the line, and sling the net."

"And if he's already through?" Wade asked.

"That," Everett said, swinging his legs inside the car and slamming the door, "just might be a blessing in disguise. Santa Ynez isn't used to things like this. It could cause a hell of a lot of trouble."

"It already has for the guy who got killed," Wade said.

"It's the living I'm worried about," Everett answered. "I don't want to have to start protecting them from themselves." Then he turned to Luke. "Come on, get us back to the station. I'm too damn mad to drive."

As Luke walked around the car, Wade leaned down to the passenger window. "I think I'll see if I can get any more out of our friend Amos."

"Give it a try. But you better play good-guy this time, because I don't think he's going to be too pleased to see you coming."

"Right. Catch you later."

The sheriff's car pulled away, followed almost immediately by the ambulance. Wade walked slowly across to Amos Clements' house, unable to avoid glancing at the spot where the victim had lain.

Once across the street, he was confronted by two teenagers casually leaning on their bicycles.

"Some guy got wasted by a car, huh?" The boy who asked the question couldn't have been much more than fourteen.

"Yeah, that's right." Wade wanted to shake some sense into the mop-haired kid, but he managed to hold his temper.

"Think you'll catch the driver?" the other one asked.

"We're doing our best. Now why don't you shove off? There's nothing left to see here."

"There's the spot," the mop-haired one said.

"What?"

"The spot where he died. I've never seen anything like that before."

"Me either," the other boy said.

Wade felt the anger coursing through his body. "And you think it'd be fun?"

"Well . . . not fun, really. Just somethin' to tell the guys about. Nothing ever happens around here, you know?"

"Is that so bad?"

The mop-haired boy shrugged. "I guess not."

"Then why don't you both get on to school and be thankful it's not part of either one of you that's soaking into the dirt across the road?"

They looked at each other, obviously bored with their mini-lecture, and pedaled off.

Wade climbed the steps to Amos' house, knowing full well that if he got inside, the two boys would almost surely be back to look at "the spot."

He rapped on the screen door and Bertha came to answer it. The drapes on the front windows were drawn and she stood well back from the door her face partially obscured in the shadows.

"Morning, Bertha. Sorry to disturb you, but I'd like to speak with Amos if I could."

"He said he didn't want to see anybody." Her voice was apologetic, yet tinged with fear.

"I understand that, but this is official business."

"Oh, well, I'll tell him, but I really don't think he's up to it. It's been quite a strain on him."

"I'm sure it has; I won't take up much of his time."

"I'll get him." She turned hesitantly and left him waiting on the porch.

It wasn't long before Wade could hear the sounds of an argument coming from the rear bedroom, and then Amos made his way noisily to the front door.

"I thought I told you I was done talking!" His breath was fresh with whiskey.

"I know you did; I just came by to apologize for the way I came down on you out there. I guess we all got a little uptight."

"That shit ain't gonna get you anywhere with me! I told you what I saw, and that's that, understand?"

"I understand, Amos. But a man's been killed, murdered just as sure as if someone put a bullet in his head. And you're the only witness. Anything you can remember—*anything*—no matter how insignificant it may seem to you, might turn out to be just the thing we need to nail this guy. And I know you want him caught just as much as we do."

"Why the hell should it make any difference to me?"

"Come on, Amos, you're the one who called us, aren't you?"

"Yeah, I'm the one, and as far as I'm concerned, it's turning out to be one of the biggest goddam mistakes I ever made. Now get your ass off my porch."

"Jesus! What's with you, anyway? There's a killer on the loose out there, and he's got one of the most lethal weapons ever invented—a car! How many more people does he have to run over before you'll try to give us a little help? Supposing it was your wife he'd hit? Or your son Jimmy? It could have been, you know. Just like it could have been you or me or anybody else

in town. So get off it, Amos, and do something worth-
while for once in your life!"

The veins on the side of Wade's head stood out, blue
and bulging. He stared hard at Amos, waiting for an
answer, watching his dull gray eyes through the dirty
screen door.

"You want some information?" Amos finally said.

"You know I do."

"Then listen good: as of this minute, you're tres-
passing on private property, and if you plan to come
back here again, you damn well better have the papers
to back it up."

He slammed the front door in Wade's face. Moments
later, walking back across the road, past "the spot" the
two boys had been so eager to see, Wade thought about
the driver of the car, the dead young man, and his own
rage and frustration at Amos Clements' blind obsti-
nacy, and it occurred to him that the desire to take another's life was a deceptively easy thing to conjure.

V

Half an hour later, the Santa Ynez police station was brimming with activity. The day shift was all present and accounted for: Chas, a powerfully built, full-blooded Navajo; Ray Mott; Fats; Ashberry; Donna at the switchboard; and Denson, MacGruder, and several others. Luke was at his desk, the telephone receiver wedged between his shoulder and neck, his hands busily pecking something out on his typewriter. A plastic bag on the upper right-hand corner of the desk held the personal effects of the young hitchhiker.

Hanging up the phone, Luke pulled the paper from the typewriter and moved to Wade's desk, where Everett stood waiting.

"Got the statistics on the boy?" Everett asked routinely.

"Statistics are for files," Luke said, "and we're a long way from closing this one. But for what it's worth, his name was John Norris; he was twenty-two, a music major at UCLA, liberal arts minor."

"UCLA?" Wade interrupted. "The kid was a long way from home."

"Not really," Luke continued. "His residence was Snedens Landing, Palisades, New York. He was hitching home for a visit."

"What about his parents?" Everett asked.

"Father's name is William Norris. He's in international reinsurance. Whatever that is."

"Sounds important," Wade said.

Luke released the paper and it settled softly on Wade's desk. While Everett picked up the sheet and scanned the information, Luke stood stoically by.

"What about L.A.P.D.?" Everett asked. "They show anything on him?"

"They're running it, but I doubt it. Palisades already checked in; he's clean over there."

"Well, I guess all that leaves is the dirty work," Everett said. "Call up William Norris." He handed the paper back to Luke.

"Thanks a hell of a lot," Luke said, and he moved off toward his desk.

"Let me make the call," Wade said when Luke was out of earshot.

"Why? Don't you think he can handle it?"

"Sure he can handle it. But it might get to him."

"Wouldn't it get to you to call up a man and tell him his son's been killed?"

"That's not the point."

"Oh, yes it is, Wade. Look, I don't like being hard-nosed any more than the next guy, and I know Luke's had his problems. But I need men I can depend on— all the time. He's been standing on his own for five years now. Let's let him keep it up."

Their conversation was cut short when Chas ambled over.

"Any word from Daigler County?" Everett asked.

"Yeah, but you're not gonna like it."

"So what else is new? Let's hear it."

"Sheriff Papez says he'd appreciate a little more information as to what the hell they're supposed to be looking for. And that's a quote."

"Well, you tell him he's got just as much as I do. And he damn well better stop everything on four wheels that's black, dark gray, navy blue, and anything else he can think of." Everett paused and raised his voice. "That goes the same for everyone here. I want everybody on the street. Now, this is a small town and we all know that the word's bound to get out. But if you're asked, the official answer is that we're looking for a hit-and-run driver. And any man who takes it on himself to go beyond that is going to be pulling graveyard shift for a good long time."

"What about a description of the car?" Fats asked. "Can we give that out?"

"Not a bad idea. But they're to check in with us immediately if they see anything. I sure as hell don't need any half-assed hero bucking for two columns in the newspaper. . . . Any other questions?"

Nobody spoke.

"Okay, then, let's get to work."

The officers filed out. As Wade passed by Luke's desk, he was just picking up the phone to call John Norris' father. Wade gave his buddy a playful shot to the shoulder.

"Meet you at the car."

Luke nodded, double-checked the number on the I.D. sheet, and began to dial.

William Norris was a man who valued his time almost as much as his money and was rarely, if ever, seen indulging either in what he considered unproductive ventures. So when his secretary announced that he had a call from the sheriff's department in Santa Ynez, Utah, his reaction was one of mild surprise followed by immediate refusal.

"Handle it for me, Mrs. Singleton; I don't know anyone in Utah."

"He says it's highly urgent and quite personal."

Her reply drew a sharp glance over the top of his steel-rimmed bifocals. This would have been answer enough for most secretaries, but Estelle Singleton held her ground. Before she'd "come aboard," as Norris liked to put it, he'd run through five secretaries—including two men—in a little less than ten months. Estelle had been made well aware of that before she'd been hired. That had been two years ago, and in the interval she'd become something of a legend among the office personnel, executive and otherwise.

Norris sighed and closed the portfolio that lay on his cherrywood desk.

"Line three," Estelle said, and left him to his call.

Norris picked up the phone impatiently and spoke in the brusque tone of someone who didn't like being interrupted by strangers, even if it was the sheriff's department.

"Yes? What is it?"

"Mr. William Norris?"

"Of course it is. What do you want?"

"This is Deputy Sheriff Johnson in Santa Ynez, Utah."

"I've never done business in Utah, Sheriff. Are you sure you have the right William Norris?"

"I'm afraid so, sir. It's about your son, John."

Norris paused, and when he resumed the conversation his voice was a little more civil. "What seems to be the trouble? Is John in some kind of difficulty?"

"I'm sorry to have to be the one to tell you, sir, but your son is dead. Killed in a hit-and-run accident."

Norris' facial muscles went slack and the lead on his gold mechanical pencil snapped on the scratch pad.

"Jesus. Are you positive?"

"As positive as we can be under the circumstances. We have his student I.D. card and an expired driver's license. The coroner's office would like you to forward his dental records for final confirmation, but please don't get your hopes up. It never pays in situations like this."

"Sheriff . . what did you say your name was?" The words came out haltingly.

"Deputy Sheriff Johnson, sir." It wasn't hard for Luke to imagine the mixture of shock and disbelief that had settled over the man.

"Were there any witnesses?"

"Only one."

"Did he get a description of the car? The license number?"

"It's all very vague, Mr. Norris."

"Except for the fact that my son is dead. That's not vague, is it, Sheriff?"

"No sir."

"And what are you doing about it?"

"Everything we can, sir."

"I'll believe that when the sonofabitch who killed my boy is brought to justice."

"Please, Mr. Norris, I know this is painful for you, but there's something I have to ask you." Luke felt like a talking manual, but there was no way something like this could be handled humanely.

"Well?" Norris was fighting to maintain control. "Ask your question."

Luke sighed and plunged ahead. "Do you know of any enemies your son may have had? Anyone who disliked him enough to want to see harm come to him?"

"What are you talking about? I thought you said it was hit-and-run."

"It was. Definitely. But there was also evidence to suggest that it wasn't an accident."

"Are you trying to tell me my son may have been murdered?"

"No sir; I'm only saying that any information you might have could conceivably be of help in our investigation."

"John . . ." Norris' voice was cracking. "John was a well-liked young man. If he had any enemies, I can assure you they weren't of his making."

"I see."

"Do you, Sheriff? Was it your son who died under the wheels of that car?"

"Of course not. I'm sorry."

"I'm not asking for your sympathy. I'm asking you to do your job. And if your negligence allows John's killer to escape, I'm going to make it my personal responsibility to see that your entire department is brought to its knees and stripped of its authority. Believe that, because I'm not a man to make idle threats."

"I'm sure that you're not, Mr. Norris."

"Is there anything else?"

"Only that once we've received the dental records, we'll be in touch with you about arrangements for transporting the body."

"Just make sure that you call me at this number. I don't want you disturbing my wife."

"Yes sir; I'll make a note of it."

Norris hung up the phone slowly, the sound of the dial tone fading away as he moved the receiver from his ear. He reached for the intercom unit on his desk, his movements a dreamlike mime of reality.

When Estelle Singleton heard the voice at the other

end of the line tell her to cancel the day's appointments, she barely recognized it as belonging to William Norris.

Luke sat at his desk, thinking about the phone conversation, and about Everett's threat of a graveyard shift. But the graveyard shift didn't bother him. Darkness was easy to take; it gave him a chance to be alone. Of course, the daylight didn't haunt him now the way it once had, when he'd been able to see the worthlessness that surrounded him. People, he'd been wont to say back then, were the curse of the human race. But that had been a long time ago, and it was an old problem that he had to keep in check.

So he pushed himself up from his desk and walked outside to meet Wade.

VI

Wade drove as he and Luke made endless passes through the town, crisscrossing the limits of Santa Ynez. Their conversation was sparse, both of them waiting for the radio to crackle and announce that someone had spotted the black car.

Though Santa Ynez was hardly a violent town, it had had its encounters with violence, just as everyplace else had. In fact, in its makeup—its traditions, its fears, its aspirations—it was a town not unlike thousands of others that dot the country. Santa Ynez was Model America, no better or worse than the people who inhabited it. Wade could even remember two other hit-and-runs in his years with the department. Actually, neither case had been much of a nut to crack, and on both occasions they'd caught the suspect within twenty-four hours. Horrified by what they'd done, the drivers had panicked and simply fled blindly, leaving trails that begged to be followed.

But this was different. Those people had been operating in what was almost a state of shock. They'd been running from themselves more than from anything else, and when they'd been apprehended, they'd been glad that it was all over. They'd taken lives, and they'd been numbed by their actions.

Not so this time. Now Wade wasn't hunting a frightened, pitiful specimen whose world had suddenly been turned inside out by too much booze or a problem at the office or a fight with his wife that had made his reflexes just a second too slow. No, this time he and Luke and all the others were tracking a hunter. They were all potential victims, and while the odds said that the car and its driver were probably long gone by now, the one thing they couldn't afford to do was to take anything for granted.

"Dispatch to twenty-two. Come in, twenty-two." The radio jarred the silence and Luke quickly handled the call.

"This is twenty-two. Go ahead, Donna."

"Everett asked me to pass the word to you. L.A.P.D. just reported in on the Norris boy."

"What do they show?"

"Nothing. Not even a traffic ticket. In fact, DMV reports he hasn't owned a car for the past three months. That explains why he was hitching."

"Thanks, Donna."

"Sorry it wasn't any better. How's it going out there?"

"Quiet. Very quiet."

"Hang in there, fellas. Dispatch out."

Luke replaced the mike in the dashboard bracket and cursed in frustration. "Shit. That's just great. No leads, no nothing."

"Did you really expect anything?" Wade asked as he stopped at a traffic signal near the town's modest shopping center.

"I guess not. But that still leaves us with one big question: why was John Norris killed? That guy didn't pick him off just for kicks."

"What makes you so sure it was a guy? Amos never said who was driving; all he saw was the car."

"Jesus," Luke said, "I never thought of that. But why a woman?"

"The kid was hitching, right? Maybe she picked him west of here and he decided to get more than a free ride out of the deal. It *has* been known to happen. Wouldn't even have to be rape. Maybe she just woke up the next morning, found him long gone, and decided to track him down and get even."

"God save us from people," Luke said disgustedly.

"Hey, it's just a theory. Don't get yourself all worked up." The light changed and they pulled away. "How about we swing by the school and see if the girls are out?"

"Sounds good. I'm about ready to see black cars on every corner."

Wade headed across town to the elementary school.

Luke fell silent, concentrating heavily on something.

"What's on your mind?" Wade finally asked.

"I think we should have Ev check it out."

"Check what out?"

"Your idea about a woman driving the car."

"*If* she was raped and *if* she reported it. That's a real longshot."

"Have we got anything else to go on?"

"Why are you so interested in a motive? If the car's in our county, we'll pull the bastard in. If it's not, it's out of our hands."

"Is that all it means to you? Either we spot the car or we don't?"

"You know better than that. I'm just trying to tell you that if you let this thing get to you, you're gonna get yourself in trouble."

"You still don't think I can handle it, do you? After all this time."

"I'm sorry. I just don't want to see you slip back, that's all."

"Yeah, okay. Let's forget it. We'll never find that car anyway, and we both know it."

"Daigler's got the word too. There's still a chance it might turn up."

"Two counties against one black car," Luke said. "Sure seems like the odds should be in our favor."

"Then relax. If it's out there, we'll get it. And if we do, then you'll have your motive for Norris' death."

"Yeah," Luke said bitterly, "lucky me."

The young boy beat furiously on his big bass drum. He was surrounded by six or seven other children, each with an instrument, and together they were engaged in what Lauren liked to refer to as a "free musical exercise." In this case, they were murdering a rousing Sousa march, and enjoying every minute of it.

The rest of the band members sat on the grass, together with fifty or sixty other children, all clapping their hands joyfully to the somewhat erratic beat of the music.

Lauren loved working with these children. After her formal training in the east, she'd sent out dozens of résumés to elementary schools, not caring where she had to move as long as the atmosphere seemed right. And the first time she'd driven through Santa Ynez, she'd known that it was where she wanted to stay. She'd been tired of big cities; every day they were turning more and more into armed camps, the people becoming paranoid about even the simplest acts of friendship and courtesy.

Her interview with the school principal, Miss McDonald, had gone extremely well; the woman had been unable to contain her enthusiasm at the chance of landing someone with Lauren's background.

Two weeks later she'd had a signed contract and had been making arrangements for a down payment on a small house on the outskirts of town. But, like all ideal situations, this one had turned out to be something less than it had appeared on the surface.

Miss McDonald, it seemed, was not the most tolerant of individuals. In fact, her attitudes in certain areas were not so much conservative as they were out-and-out primitive. And that sunny morning, as Lauren watched her striding purposefully across the athletic field toward the impromptu band concert, she knew she was in for a bad time.

Miss McDonald arrived on the scene just as the Sousa march came to a vibrant halt—to the wild applause of everyone but the principal.

She tapped Lauren briskly on the shoulder. "Miss Humphries, I'd like to speak with you for a moment."

"Sure . . . what's up?"

Miss McDonald frowned. "In private, if you don't mind."

"Whatever you say." Lauren turned to the band members. "Take a break, kids; then we'll all rehearse the march together."

"You mean the *real* way?" one of the children called out.

"If you think you can remember how it goes."

The children laid down their instruments and took off to play as Lauren and Miss McDonald walked a few feet away.

"What can I do for you?" Lauren asked casually.

The principal handed her a sheet of rolled-up art paper. "I'd like to know precisely what this is."

Lauren unrolled the paper and couldn't help smiling

broadly as she looked at a sketch of what was obviously supposed to be herself, nude, standing at the head of the classroom, blackboard pointer in hand.

"Do you see what I mean?" Miss McDonald said gravely.

"I certainly do, and I think it's terribly sweet. He made me at least a thirty-six D. But he really didn't put enough contrast in the shaded areas, don't you think?"

The principal drew herself up to her full, ungainly height of six-feet-four.

"Then you're admitting that's a picture of *you?*"

"Sure looks that way, doesn't it?"

"I must say I'm surprised."

"So am I; he's pretty good, although overly generous with his proportions."

"Then you know who did it?"

"I'd just prefer to think it was a boy, wouldn't you? It's a lot healthier that way."

"And you think it's healthy for a thirteen-year-old boy to imagine his teacher naked? Is that what you're trying to tell me?"

"Thirteen-year-old boys are renowned for their imaginations, Miss McDonald. And the human body, especially where the opposite sex is concerned, is a perfectly normal area of consideration."

"I'm afraid I find that your attitude in this matter leaves a great deal to be desired."

"You hired me as a music teacher, not an art critic."

"Whatever I hired you as, Miss Humphries, be assured that I can also fire you."

She grabbed the sketch from Lauren's hand and blustered off across the field.

As Lauren stood looking after her, Margie Johnson, Luke's wife, walked over. A voluptuous brunette of thirty, Margie was the girls' athletic instructor at the school. Her working uniform consisted of navy-blue shorts that showed off the fine lines of her legs, a white T-shirt, tennis shoes, and a silver whistle on a chain around her neck. Her perky disposition had endeared her to Lauren from the first day they'd met, and their relationship had been cemented even further by the fact that Wade and Luke were such good friends.

"Hi. What's up?" Margie could see that Lauren was disturbed about something.

"Another run-in with our fearless leader."

Margie glanced over her shoulder at the departing figure of Miss McDonald.

"Forget it," Margie said. "It's happened before; it'll happen again. There isn't anyone on the faculty who hasn't had a turn or two with her."

"Maybe, but I seem to be getting elected quite a lot lately."

"Good. The time to start worrying is when she *doesn't* bother you."

"I suppose."

"What was it about, anyway?"

"It seems I have a secret admirer."

"A juicy little love letter, huh?"

"Better than that: an extremely flattering sketch of me—in the nude."

Margie couldn't suppress a smile. "My God, you really rate, don't you? Any idea who did it?"

"Not really, but McDonald would love to know. You know, Margie, sometimes I wonder if I made a mistake in coming here."

"Come on, you're a hell of a good music teacher and you get along marvelously with the kids. So what it comes down to is that you've got a good job and a lousy boss, which makes you no worse off than several million other people."

The sound of a horn interrupted their conversation and they looked toward the street; there were Wade and Luke on the other side of the chain-link fence that bordered the athletic field.

"Hey, there's the fellas. Better not tell Wade about the picture—he's liable to get insanely jealous."

"Maybe it wouldn't be such a bad idea."

"Don't worry, kid, he's just a little gun-shy, that's all."

Margie waved at their patrol car. "Come on, let's go. And don't forget to wish Luke a happy anniversary."

An active girl by nature, she jogged over to the car at a brisk clip, Lauren trailing behind.

Luke brightened visibly when he saw Margie, her ample breasts bobbing up and down as she ran. Reaching the patrol car, she immediately bent down and gave him a kiss, then looked across at Wade.

"So how's it going?"

"Things could be worse, I suppose," Wade said just as Lauren walked up.

"That's a great line for me to come in on." She blew a kiss at Wade, then smiled down at Luke. "By the way, happy anniversary."

Luke looked at Margie, then flashed a half-embarrassed grin.

"Hey, wait a minute," Lauren said. "I thought you two were married on New Year's Day?"

"We were," Margie answered. By now, everyone was smiling except Lauren.

"Okay, what's going on that I don't know about?"

"I didn't say it was *our* anniversary," Margie said impishly. "It's Luke's."

"Luke's?" Lauren was definitely puzzled. "Come on, gang, somebody clue me in."

"This is my fifth dry year." There was a sure trace of pride in Luke's voice.

Lauren was astonished. "You mean you . . . I had no idea."

"Don't worry, you're not going to hurt my feelings."

"And it's been five years? I think that's wonderful."

"So does everybody else in town," Wade said, " 'cause when he was drunk, you never knew what the hell he was gonna do. Damn near burned down his father's church once."

"You're kidding!"

Luke was laughing and shaking his head. "No, it's the truth. And believe me, it caused quite a few problems."

"Now you're just a dull old boy," Margie said.

"With five years of ginger ale under my belt. Wanna go back to the good old days, honey?"

"Not on your life. I'll do the drinking for both of us. Besides, there're certain things you do a lot better when you're sober."

"Daddy! Daddy!" They all looked up to see Debra and Lynn Marie running excitedly toward them. For a frightening moment they thought something was wrong, but the girls' faces were beaming.

"What in the world are you two all worked up about?" Wade asked.

They had to wait to catch their breath. Debbie spoke first, the words tumbling out one on top of another.

"We're gonna get to be cowgirls in the parade!"

"Both of us!" Lynn Marie interjected. "Isn't that great?"

"The best news I've had in a good long time," Wade said.

"They picked us because we both know how to ride," Lynn Marie said.

"And tomorrow we don't have to go to any classes because we're gonna practice—you know, staying together in line and everything." Debbie was so excited she had all she could do to keep from jumping up and down.

"You think you can keep those horses under control?" Luke asked in mock seriousness.

"Oh, sure," Lynn Marie answered quickly. "There's nothing to it."

"Just make sure the horses understand that," Wade said.

"Oh, Daddy, really." Debbie used her most adult tone of voice. "We could practically do it with our eyes closed."

"I just hope they don't boot you out when they see this," Lauren said.

"See what?" Lynn Marie asked anxiously.

"Leaving the school yard without permission."

"What if one of the teachers notices?" Margie said.

"But you're both teachers!" The girls laughed and ran off, calling goodbye as they went.

Lauren smiled after them. "Did you ever see two people so happy about anything? It's absolutely contagious."

"Then let's get the troops together tonight and have a celebration," Wade said. "After all, it's Luke's anniversary and my daughters are gonna be cowgirls. "What more of an excuse do we need?"

"Sounds good to me," Margie said.

"It's settled then," Wade continued. "I'll throw some steaks on the barbecue, Lauren can mess up a salad, and we'll have ourselves some fun."

Suddenly a man's voice filtered across the police radio.

"Twenty-two . . . twenty-two, please respond."

Luke picked up the mike and pushed in the talk-back button. "This is twenty-two; we copy."

The disembodied voice came on again, staccato with excitement. "This is Fats! We're at the north side of High Road. We got us some real bad news out here. Ev just arrived and he wants you. Pronto!"

"How about some details?"

"You'll have all the details you can stomach when you get here. Just move!"

"We're on our way. Ten-four."

Luke jammed the mike into its bracket and a pall came over the two men as Wade slammed the car into gear and sped off down the street.

Neither Margie nor Lauren spoke as they walked back to the athletic field. Even in a small town like Santa Ynez, emergency calls weren't all that unusual. But the agitation in Fats's voice, and the expression on the men's faces as they'd received the call, told the girls that something out of the ordinary was going on, and it left them both with a nagging chord of anxiety that neither could shake.

When they reached the field, Margie jogged listlessly over to her gym class.

Lauren gathered the band together for a rehearsal, but when she gave the downbeat for the Sousa march her mind definitely wasn't on the music.

VII

When they approached their destination on High Road, Wade and Luke were slowed almost to a stop by a procession of cars: children hanging out of windows, parents craning their necks, all in an expectant, concerted effort to get a glimpse of whatever it was that was causing the bottleneck.

Unable to pass the cars because of the series of blind curves in the road at this point, Wade gave the wheel a good swat with the heel of his hand.

"What the hell do they think they're gonna see?" Luke said disgustedly. "A goddamn massacre?"

"Why not? After all, they need a few good stories to bring back home."

"And some poor bastard lying by the side of the road makes for much better dinner conversation than the scenery?"

"You guessed it."

As they rounded a curve, two deputies came into view, unsuccessfully urging the cars to speed up and be on their way.

Wade pulled over and they got out. Just then, one of the tourists pulled in behind him. Wade and Luke moved to the car immediately, Wade stopping the driver's door just as it was opening.

"Keep it moving, sir."

"We're not blocking anything." The man wore a garishly printed sport shirt. Beside him, his wife was in the process of snapping a film cartridge into a camera. In the back seat, an extremely overweight boy of nine or ten peered out at Wade through the fleshy slits of his eyes.

"We want to get some pictures," the woman said.

"There're plenty of other spots down the road where you can do that."

"Yeah," the man said, "but something's going on here."

"It sure is," Luke answered. "And you're in our way; so move it out. Now."

"This is a public road," the wife snapped. "We have every right to be here."

"Look! Blood!" The boy's bloated hand pointed toward the stone guardrail.

"Is that right?" the driver asked excitedly. "Is that what it is?"

"I really don't know," Wade said. "But I'll tell you one thing: either you start this car and get out of here, or I'll see to it that you and your family get a free ride into our nice little town."

"On what grounds? We haven't done anything."

"Oh, we'll think of something," Luke said. "We're real good at that around here."

The driver looked from one to the other, then slammed his door shut.

"What are you doing?" his wife cried shrilly.

"I wanna see!" the boy whined. "I wanna see!"

The driver looked hard at Wade. "Make you feel important, pushing taxpayers around like this?"

Wade jerked his thumb toward the road and the driver reluctantly pulled away.

"Nothin' wrong with the human race that a shortage

of people wouldn't cure," Luke said as they walked across to the crimson-streaked railing.

The mangled bicycle half and the shredded piece of plaid blouse lay at their feet. Together, they leaned over and looked down into the canyon.

It was a jagged, merciless drop of three hundred feet. And on an outcropping of rock, splayed out like a discarded puppet, lay the mutilated body of young Suzie. A few feet away, the rest of her bike glinted in the bright sunlight.

Chas, standing solitary guard over the grim scene, looked up, saw Wade and Luke, and waved them down. They could see other official vehicles parked below Chas, at the base of the canyon, and could recognize the stout silhouette of Fats.

Luke moved his lips in a brief, silent prayer as they made their way back to their car.

An obscure dirt fire road was the only access from their position on High Road, and as clouds of dust flared around the windshield, neither man would speak, as if leaving the probable cause of the girl's death unspoken would somehow prevent it from being real.

At the bottom of the canyon, about fifty feet below the shelf of rock that held the body, a broad stream flowed peacefully by. Everett sat under a large shade tree, talking with a deputy and taking notes. He glanced up at the sound of Wade's approaching car; then Chas's deep, rich voice knifed through the air.

"Hey, Fats! I need a . . . bag or something to get her down in."

Fats turned to Wally, the ambulance attendant. "You guys carry any body bags?"

"Jesus." Wally ambled off toward the ambulance.

"Wally's gettin' em," Fats called up to Chas, who raised a brawny arm in affirmation.

Wade pulled up next to the ambulance just as Wally removed two heavy-duty trash bags from beneath the driver's seat. Joe, the other attendant, carried a wire litter.

"We gotta stop meeting like this," Wally said as Wade stepped from the sheriff's car. It was a poor attempt at a joke, and he knew it as soon as the words were out of his mouth. "Sorry, but it's been one hell of a lousy day, and it isn't even noon yet."

"Forget it," Wade said. He and Luke walked over to Everett, who stood up when he saw them coming.

In the background, they could hear Fats calling out to Chas: "How many do you want?"

"Just one, if it's a big bag."

Everett grimaced at the exchange.

"What's happening?" Luke said, his face ashen. "What the hell's going on around here?"

"I wish I knew," Everett answered. "Believe me, I wish to God I knew." He turned to Wade. "You ever seen Dr. Pullbrook's daughter Susan?"

"I've met her a few times."

"Think you'd know her if you saw her again?"

"I suppose." His answer was barely audible.

"Christ, Ev." Luke was numbed by the implication. "She couldn't have been more than, what? Nineteen? Twenty?"

"Somewhere in there," Everett answered. "She went off Thursday with her boyfriend—a guy named Pete Keil—they were on a bicycle trip to soak up some nature. You know the kind of thing."

"That's impossible," Luke said firmly.

"Look, I don't like to think of the girl being dead any more than you do, but . . ."

"I'm talking about Pete," Luke interrupted.

"What about him?"

"The kid's my neighbor. He told me he had to be in Ogden on Thursday."

"So maybe he changed his mind," Wade said.

Luke shook his head. "Listen, a few years ago his father died and Pete kind of took a shine to me. Anyway, he had a job interview in Ogden on Thursday. I know because I gave him a letter of recommendation."

"Do you know for a fact that he showed up?" Everett asked.

"I'm only a deputy eight hours a day. The rest of the time, I trust people."

"Hey, I'm just trying to get a line on this thing, that's all."

Everett flung a small stone he'd been holding into the stream and took a few steps away from the deputies, standing with his back to them. His cheeks burned with anger and frustration, and in spite of himself he found that he was questioning his capabilities. That was something he'd resolved never to do after he'd succeeded Wade's father as sheriff, but it was a hard resolution to keep. They were different men and these were different times, but the comparison was always there, waiting to be drawn, and not just by Everett, but by the department and the town itself. Wade Parent, Sr., had been a man in control, whether presiding over a Sunday dinner or cajoling an abusive drunk back to the station for some strong coffee and an unofficial night's rest. What would he have done in a situation like this? But, Everett told himself, that was a moot question. *He* was sheriff, and *he* was the one with two dead bodies on his hands.

"What about an estimated time of death?" At Luke's question Everett turned back to his deputies.

"From what Chas saw of the body, he thinks some time this morning. Maybe four or five hours ago."

"That would put it just after sun-up," Wade said.

"Right. With a deserted road and no witnesses."

"So we have no way of knowing if it was the same car or not," Luke said.

"Be reasonable," Everett said. "There can't be *two* guys running around who'd do something like this."

"But it *could* have been an accident. A drunk could have done this and never even known what happened. That much I can guarantee you."

"Okay, then why hasn't the Keil boy come forward to report it?"

"Because he wasn't here," Luke said.

"The entire area been gone over?" Wade asked.

"Thoroughly, and no sign of anybody," Everett answered.

"Then that settles it," Luke said. "She was alone."

"To be honest with you, Luke, I just don't know what to think."

"Then give him the benefit of the doubt."

Everett grinned. "You always this stubborn?"

"Drives Margie nuts."

"Well, tell her I just joined the club." He continued, "All right, I want roadblocks on the interstate, Casper, Webster, Delaware, and the desert side, too. No cars —black, gray, or blue—get in or out. I want this area sealed off just as tight as we can get it. Now, let's move."

The men dispersed, Wade and Luke walking back to their car. They arrived just as the attendants were slamming the tailgate on the ambulance.

"How long before we can have a positive I.D.?" Wade called out.

Wally shrugged. "Pullbrook's going to get the first look at her. I sure don't want to be around when that happens."

"Yeah, I know what you mean. See you later."

"I hope not; this is getting to be a routine I don't particularly enjoy."

Wally and Joe climbed into the ambulance and drove away.

Wade kicked at the ground. "Shit, ten years of giving out traffic tickets and then all this in one day. I don't know when I've felt so goddamn helpless."

"Beginning to get to you too, isn't it?"

"Yeah. I suppose I should take my own advice."

"Sometimes that's not so easy to do. I know; I'm a past master at ignoring my better judgment."

The two men got into the car and drove away, following the gentle stream back toward the road.

VIII

Wade and Luke settled themselves in opposite sides of a booth in a small diner just down the street from the sheriff's office. Mechanically, they each grabbed a dog-eared menu from behind the sugar dispenser and stared blankly at the list of items.

Sunlight spilled across their table and Luke turned to look out the window. Its tinted coating was bathing the parking lot and the street in a pale spill of green. He was trying to think of nothing, to lose himself in a vacant daydream, when his attention was diverted by the clatter of silverware being placed in front of him. He looked up and saw Dora, a sturdy, dark-haired waitress in her late thirties.

"What about it, fellas? Ready to order?"

"I'll take a cheeseburger and fries," Wade said. "And some iced tea."

Luke returned his menu to its holder behind the sugar. "Just coffee."

"Eat," Wade urged. "It'll do you good."

Luke managed a feeble smile. "Yes, Mother. . . . I'll have a burger, no onions," he said to Dora.

She jotted down the order and looked at Wade. "I heard about that hitchhiker this morning. What a lousy thing. Somebody said he was run over four or five times. That true?"

"Where did you hear that?" Luke asked.

"I don't know, just around. Gossip travels in and out of here all day long."

"Don't believe everything you hear," Wade said. "The guy was hit and that's all there is to it. Okay?"

"Sure, fellas. Whatever you say."

"Why the cover-up?" Luke asked after she'd gone to hand in the order. "Amos is bound to have the story all over town anyway."

"Amos is also drunk half the time," Wade said. "And as long as we can keep them guessing, the better off we'll be. Besides, we're going to have enough trouble on our hands after the word gets out about the Pullbrook girl."

Luke didn't answer, but stared over Wade's shoulder toward the door of the diner. Wade swiveled in his seat and saw Dr. Pullbrook coming down the aisle in their direction.

Attired in a gray three-piece suit, he held himself erect and walked with a steady gait that brought him to their table before either of them had come up with the slightest idea of how to handle the situation. They started to stand up, but he motioned them back into their seats.

"I've just come from the coroner's office." His voice was strained and the battle to conceal his emotions showed on his face. "I'd like to sit down and talk with you."

Wade slid over next to the window, dragging his napkin and silverware with him. He felt awkward and out of place as the doctor sat down beside him.

Luke kept his head down, tracing invisible designs on his paper napkin with the handle of his spoon.

"I'm sorry, Doctor. We're all sorry." Wade found the words difficult to speak. "I want you to know on behalf of the entire department that we're doing everything we can."

"Doing everything you can," Pullbrook said mechanically. "Those seem to be patented phrases in medicine and police work, only until today I didn't realize how goddamn useless the words were." He swallowed back his grief and continued. "I was just talking to Everett over at the station. From what he tells me, you don't have much to work with."

"I'm afraid not," Wade said.

Dora came by with the coffee and iced tea. "Hello, Doctor. Can I get you something?"

He looked up at her blankly. "No, nothing."

"Your burgers'll be up in a minute, fellas," she said and hurried off to another table.

"You know," Pullbrook said through his exhaustion, "I'm a Mormon by religion and a physician by calling. Both of those things are supposed to make me better prepared to accept death than most people. But neither one seems to be doing me any good. All I can think about is how I'm going to tell my wife. Maybe if I could tell her *why* this happened . . ." His words trailed off into silence.

Wade took a sip of his iced tea, wishing he had something concrete to offer. Finally, he could stall no longer.

"What can I say, Doctor? So far the only link is the victims' ages. They were both young. But that could just as easily be a coincidence."

"Or a symbol," Luke said.

"Of what?" The doctor knew it was quite probably an exercise in futility, but somehow trying to pin a reason to his daughter's death helped to ease his despair.

"Maybe I'm grasping at straws," Luke said, "but the

victims were free and independent. They were out on their own and taking life as it came, flaunting convention. Their ability to do that may have some connection with why they were killed. Does that make any sense to you?"

"It makes as much sense as anything," Wade interrupted, trying to inject a note of hope into the conversation. "And believe me, if the guy's anywhere in this county, we'll nail him."

"But the fact is," Pullbrook said slowly, forcing himself to confront the reality, "he could be well beyond your roadblocks, hours away, isn't that right?"

"Yes sir, that's a possibility."

"He's still here," Luke said, "and I'd be willing to bet on it."

There was a long pause before Dr. Pullbrook spoke, a twinge of the professional reaching through his emotions. "If you're right, if he comes back and kills again, then you've got an epidemic on your hands, just as surely as if people were dropping from the plague. And if that happens, then you're going to have the whole town to fight, not just a madman in a black car." He massaged the ridge of bone above his eyes with his left hand. "I want to find out who killed my daughter, and why, but if that means other people will have to die, I'd rather have my questions remain unanswered."

"Maybe they won't have to," Wade said.

"Maybe," Pullbrook said softly, and he stood up. "Thanks for talking to me. Thank you both. Now . . . now I have to go home."

He turned and left just as Dora arrived with their food. She set down the plates and a bottle of ketchup, and tore the check off her pad and laid it on the table.

"Enjoy your lunch," she said cheerfully.

* * *

Half an hour later, with Wade waiting in the patrol car, Luke entered the local branch of the Zion National Bank. Since it was still the lunch hour, it was fairly crowded; he scanned the row of teller's cages but caught no sight of Alice Keil.

Both the manager and the assistant manager were out to lunch, so his inquiries led him to the operations officer, Miss Wallace, who had the unmistakable look of a career woman.

"Can I help you?" Even her tone was an ideal of well-modulated efficiency.

"I'd like to speak to Alice Keil. It's official business."

"I see." She glanced at a roster taped to the wall beside her desk. "Alice is on her lunch break."

"Does that mean she's out of the bank?"

"Not necessarily; a lot of us bring our lunch and eat in the employees' lounge. It's really very nice."

"I'm sure it is. Can you check and see if she's there?"

"You did say it was official business?"

"That's right."

"Nothing that might embarrass the bank, I hope."

Luke tried to control his temper. "Her son may be dead. Would you call that embarrassing to the bank?"

"Oh, I'm sorry; I'll check right away."

She picked up the phone and dialed a three-digit number.

"This is Mary. Does Alice Keil happen to be up there? Fine. Send her down to my desk right away, please."

She hung up the phone, and she sounded genuinely concerned when she spoke. "What's happened to the boy?"

"We're not sure that anything's happened to him yet.

But I need some questions answered, and she's the only one who can do it."

He saw Alice descending a staircase on the opposite side of the bank. As soon as she noticed Luke, she quickened her pace.

He walked across to meet her, not wanting to discuss the situation any further in front of Miss Wallace.

"Luke, is something wrong?"

"Come on over here, Alice," he said, leading her to an empty sofa near the front door.

When they sat, she perched nervously on the edge of the cushion, her hands clasped together in her lap.

"Look, I can see that you're upset already, and I hate to be the one to put you through this, but—"

"Something's happened to Pete, hasn't it?" She cut in with the words as if they were a statement rather than a question.

"I don't know, Alice. But there's a chance he never went on that job interview up in Ogden."

Her eyes widened in amazement. "That's impossible. I mean, where else would he go?"

"He was taking the bus to Ogden, wasn't he?"

"Of course."

"Then you'd know if his bike was missing?"

She hesitated. "Not really."

"Why? Did he loan it out to someone?"

"No, it's just that Merle used to use half the garage for his workshop—he was never happier than when he was in there puttering with something—anyway, since he's been gone, I just don't like to go in there unless I have to. It's silly, I know, but in the good weather I keep the car outside. Now, why don't you just come out with whatever it is you're trying to tell me?"

Luke gave a little sigh. "Alice, do you know Dr. Pullbrook's daughter, Susan?"

"Pete's been out with her a few times; she seems like a nice enough girl. Why?"

"According to Dr. Pullbrook, Susan and Pete took off on Thursday for a bicycle trip together." Luke hesitated, and Alice gave a grateful smile of relief, jumping to conclusions before he could explain the rest.

"For God's sake, Luke Johnson, you ought to be ashamed of yourself, getting me all upset for something like that. Listen, I'm not trying to make any excuses, but I'm a woman alone and Pete's an active young man. One thing's for sure, he'd never get away on any trip like that if Merle were still alive. But this generation, it's sure a lot different from when you and I were young. And I suppose there's a lot worse things he could be out doing. Anyway, you can bet I'll let him know I'm plenty displeased when he gets back. And it wouldn't be a bad idea if the doctor had a good talk with his daughter, too. After all, it's the girl who suffers if anything goes wrong."

She glanced at her watch. "Good heavens, lunch hour's almost over and I've got half my sandwich to eat."

Reaching out, she patted Luke's hand. "Cheer up, will you? I know it was embarrassing for you to have to tell me, but these things happen. Maybe you could speak to him when he gets back. He looks up to you, you know."

She started to get up, but he grabbed her arm, half sick that he hadn't stopped her the minute she'd started talking.

"Wait a minute, Alice; there's more."

"More? They haven't even come home yet, have they? What more could there be?"

Luke moistened his lips. Then he heard himself

speaking, but the sound of his own voice seemed strangely disconnected from his body.

"We found Susan Pullbrook's body late this morning, at the bottom of High Road. We have good reason to believe she was deliberately run off the highway by a car. There was no sign of Pete—not anywhere."

The blood drained from Alice's face and she roughly pulled her arm away from Luke. Her mouth began to twitch, working in spasms to form words that couldn't, or wouldn't, come out.

He reached for her, but she slid away from him on the sofa.

"Please, Alice, we won't know anything for sure until we confirm that he didn't go to Ogden. And even then, there's always the chance that somehow he wasn't with her when it happened."

Wade walked in, stopping abruptly when he saw the two of them together. He had no choice but to go over to the sofa and announce his news.

"I just got word from the station," he said quietly. "Pete never showed in Ogden."

Alice stood up slowly, flanked by the two deputies.

"You're a liar," she said softly. Then, "Liar! Liar! Liar!" she screamed in an uncontrollable rage, flailing her clenched fists against Wade's chest.

All across the bank, people stared in the direction of the spectacle.

Luke grabbed her arms and turned her around. Alice simply stood there, trembling with fear and despair, and only vaguely aware of the click-click-click of Miss Wallace's high heels on the polished floor as she hurried across the room.

IX

Nightfall saw Wade, Luke, and several of the other deputies gathered at the station. The building itself was a stark, no-frills edifice over thirty years old, but it served its purpose well—it was functional and secure.

Inside, men were grouped in clusters in the aisles between rows of gray metal desks. Fluorescent lighting (recently installed to replace the out-of-date circular fixtures) cast a harsh light against the pale green walls. Cigarette smoke and the low, insistent hum of intense conversation drifted through the air. To the left of the main entry, between two corner windows, the inevitable coffee maker sat atop a plain wooden table, and many of the deputies held white styrofoam cups filled with its hot black liquid. The northeast corner of the rectangular room held the switchboard; it stood silent, and to a man everyone in the room hoped it would remain that way.

It had been a tension-ridden day, especially once the word of Susan Pullbrook's death had circulated. Sightings of a black car had peppered the radio dispatches —none of them had yielded anything more than dead ends and irritable citizens. And with each dry lead, Wade could see the basis of panic forming, Dr. Pullbrook's warning of "epidemic" looming as a very possible reality.

When Wade and Luke checked in, a not uncommon scene was being played out at the far end of the room, directly in front of Everett's desk, which was positioned at an angle at the rear of the room so as to command an unobstructed view of the whole station.

The Clementses were there—Amos, Bertha, and young Jimmy; all it took was one look at Bertha's bruised, swollen face to tell the familiar story and explain why she'd remained in the shadows when Wade had called on Amos at his house.

Everett got up and quickly drew Wade aside. "Since you're the senior deputy around here, you get to lay the extra duty on the fellas; I've got my hands full over there." He nodded in the direction of the Clementses.

"Thanks a lot, Chief. They're gonna love me for this."

Everett handed Wade the duty roster and flashed him a gloating smile. "I knew you wouldn't mind."

Wade grimaced as he looked at the list of long hours, the random pattern telling him it had been constructed by the luck of the draw, as fair a solution as any when it came to handing out extra assignments. What he didn't like was the fact that neither he nor Luke had drawn any overtime on the night shift; the guys were sure to get on him for that.

He walked to the center of the room, calling everybody's attention. "Okay, gang, it's good-news time."

A highly unfriendly grumble went up as the deputies gathered around.

"This is the way it comes down," Wade said. "We're gonna keep street patrols going all night long, plus the roadblocks. So far, this lunatic and his car haven't taken anybody else out that we know of, and we plan to keep it that way. Chances are the guy's long gone, but we can't afford to assume anything. I know some of you have drawn very long hours, but that can't be helped. We'll try to make it up to you as soon as we can; until then there's not a hell of a lot we can do about it."

Wade posted the roster on the bulletin board, and edged out of the way as casually as possible.

"Hey, my friend," Dalton called to Wade, "I don't see your name up here."

"Just lucky, I guess."

"How about letting some of it rub off on a poor Indian?" Chas kidded.

"Your cars are that way, gentlemen." Wade pointed to the rear door that led to the parking lot. "Enjoy your evening."

He took a lot of good-natured abuse as several of the deputies filed out; then Luke walked by.

"Hey," Wade said, "steaks at my place. Remember?"

"I'm not sure I'm in the mood to celebrate."

"It's better than sitting home with nothing to do but think."

"Why? Is forgetting about it going to change anything?"

"No, but maybe it'll help us get through it."

"You mean help *me*."

"I mean *all* of us. You think I enjoyed looking at those two kids today?"

"That's not what I said."

"Good. Then I'll see you for dinner."

Luke managed a slight smile. "Yeah, I'll be there. Meantime, I'm gonna grab a look at the armaments locker and see what we've got."

"You think it'll come to that?"

Luke's face was hard when he spoke. "I almost wish it would; I'd love a chance to blow that guy away."

He turned and walked the length of the room, pulling open the heavy door that led to the arms locker.

Inside, thick cement walls enclosed the windowless five-by-eight area. Two racks of rifles and a four-tier wooden shelf holding ammunition and flack jackets represented the entire contents of the room.

Luke stood alone and looked at the guns. There was enough fire power here to stop the black car a dozen times. What was the term the military had coined to describe something like that? Overkill, that was it. Even the modest arsenal of the Santa Ynez Sheriff's Department had entered the age of overkill. Except that the weapons were on the wall and the ammunition was on the shelf and two dead bodies were in the morgue.

Supposing, he thought, supposing he *did* have a chance to kill the driver of the car. Would he do it? Certainly he'd never killed anyone before, although death had always played a prominent role in his life— he'd been devastated by his mother's death when he was seven, scarred by his father's blistering sermons on the topic, and had fervently wished his own death when the alcohol could no longer perform its emotional anesthesia. And now death was close to him again; two young people had been blotted out of existence, and another, a boy who needed a father just as much as Luke had, would quite probably be number three. And what if there were more? Would the guns come down off the wall then? Or would it be too late? Would the car continue to take its toll like some whirlwind pestilence from the Bible?

Suddenly Luke felt very vulnerable. It was a feeling he hadn't had for quite some time. But then, he reasoned, perhaps five years wasn't nearly as long a time as he'd thought it to be.

❈　❈　❈

Wade sat on the corner of a desk, far enough away to give Everett some privacy with the Clementses—not that there were any doubts about what was going on. It was a scene that was repeated every couple of months with infuriating regularity.

Across the room, Everett was trying to reason with Bertha. Amos had moved to one of the empty chairs a few feet away, and their son, Jimmy, sat sullenly in a limbo between his parents.

"For the last time, Bertha, if you don't press charges, there's nothing I can do. That bastard can get up and walk out, and when he finally decides to come home, bombed out of his empty head, the whole thing's going to start all over again."

Her only reply was to turn slightly away from Everett.

"Look," he said in exasperation, "what about your son? You think it's doing him any good to live in a situation like this? He's a young boy; he deserves a stable home, and you're the only one who can give it to him."

He pushed a paper in front of her and held out a pen.

"Here, sign this now and it's over. Just your name is all it takes, and you can go home and relax for a change. Please, Bertha, sign it."

She shook her head no—a timid, fearful movement that was barely noticeable.

"Ah, Christ!" Everett said, throwing the pen down in disgust. "Okay," he said to Amos. "Get the hell out. But I'm not done with you. Not by a damn sight, I'm not."

Amos threw him an incensed look and stood up. Bertha moved to follow her husband, but Everett stayed her.

"Not yet," he said firmly. Then, to Amos, "Go on, move!"

Clements stood there, staring balefully at his wife. Then he turned to Everett with a hateful expression of victory that made the sheriff come very close to taking off his badge and beating the hell out of him right then and there. The message obviously came across loud and clear, because Amos suddenly turned and stormed out of the station.

Everett regained control of his temper. "You don't have to go home, Bertha. There's nothing to go home *to*. Why don't you let us put you and Jimmy up at a motel tonight? Then tomorrow we'll talk things out. Trust me; it'd be for the best."

She looked at him, and for a moment he read something in her battered, pitiful face that gave him hope. Then it was gone, and she pushed herself up from the desk, holding her hand out for Jimmy.

Everett watched them leave, shaking his head in bitter resignation, and then walked over to Wade.

"Do you believe that?" he asked quietly.

"Hard to figure," Wade answered.

"I went to school with her, you know. You couldn't meet a nicer person. But shy—God, she was painfully shy. And loyal. If she was friends with someone, it didn't make any difference what they did as far as Bertha was concerned. She'd stick by 'em no matter what. Damned ironic, isn't it? That's a trait you don't find much anymore, and all it's done for her is cause her a bundle of grief. You know, at one time, she was . . ." He paused, lost in thought, then snapped back to reality. "You got everything organized?"

"Soon as I plug the pins in," Wade said, and he moved to a relief map that hung on the wall. He began to position colored pins to coincide with the assignments on the duty roster.

As he worked, he couldn't help commenting on the day's unexpected events. "My father was sheriff here for thirty-one years, Ev. In all that time, nothing ever happened to compare to this. Today was—hell, there's just no word for it. And I hope to God I never see another one like it."

"It was different in his time," Everett said. "What happened today reflects on *our* world. We've just been lucky to escape up to now."

"Then we damn well better hurry up and get lucky again." Wade put the last pin in the map.

Everett let his eyes roam over the empty desks. The lifelessness of the room reflected in inverse proportion the magnitude of the crisis. Though no violent incidents had developed since the discovery of Susan Pullbrook's body, the threat of unbridled chaos still hung above their heads—a flash fire of emotions could still gut the town in a single, devastating sweep.

It was Everett's job to make sure that that didn't happen, and he was enough of a realist to know that the outcome would depend as much upon chance as on anything else.

"You know," he finally said, "it's just as well the Old Man isn't around to see this."

Wade nodded a silent assent. Santa Ynez had been his father's sole consuming passion—not to the exclusion of his family, but certainly to the point where they ranked a definite second. Wade knew that Everett was aware of that, and because of it the bond between the two men was a strong one.

"And now it's all been dropped in your lap," Wade said. "I sure as hell don't envy you."

"That makes two of us, but feeling sorry for ourselves isn't going to get the job done."

"You think there's anything to Pullbrook's theory?" Wade asked, glad that Everett hadn't lost his resolve.

"Who knows? You try to motivate something like this, you end up beating your head against the wall. All I want to do is catch the guy. That's the only way we're going to get our answers. Meantime, I could sure as hell use a drink. How about you?"

"I'm for that; I'll even buy."

"That sounds like the offer of a well-adjusted man. Life must be going right for you."

"I don't know that I'm the one to comment on my life," Wade said. "But I could lose this whole day in booze real easy."

"You buying or philosophizing?" Everett said gruffly. "Because you don't have the brains to do both."

The sound of footsteps caught their attention and Luke entered, barely acknowledging the other two men.

"So?" Wade called across. "What about the arms locker?"

Luke slumped at his desk. "The lock was rusty. We won't know anything about the guns without a test."

"Then we'll worry about that tomorrow," Everett said. "How about joining us across the street?" He realized his gaffe the minute he'd said it. "Sorry; I forgot."

"No sweat."

"He's five years clean today," Wade said proudly.

"No kidding? Congratulations. You've got more willpower than I do."

"As a matter of fact," Wade said, "we're having a little celebration at my place for dinner, and there's always room for one more."

"Thanks, but I think I'll stick around here for a while and make sure things ride easy."

"Go ahead and have your drink," Luke prompted. "I'll meet you at the house."

"Order me a gin and tonic," Wade said to Everett. "I'll be along in a minute."

Everett nodded and walked toward the front door of the station as Wade crossed to Luke's desk.

"Listen, you sure you're okay?"

"Why not? I've watched two young kids be scooped up and hauled away to the morgue, talked to both their parents, and told the widowed mother of a third that her boy's probably next on the list. Why the hell shouldn't I be okay?"

The two looked at each other in silence; it was an argument for which Wade had no rebuttal. "See you at the house," he said.

Just outside the door, Everett was absorbed in something going on down the street. "How's that for a nice end to your day?"

Wade looked off to his right. About a hundred feet down the dimly lit street, the Clements family stood beside their battered pickup truck. It was obvious that they were arguing, and from their gestures it appeared as if Bertha was trying to convince Amos to get into the truck. Finally he banged his fist on the hood in a rage.

Defeated and dreading another public scene, Bertha helped Jimmy into the truck and drove away.

Everett was incensed. "That sonofabitch! Threatening his wife and kid like that! Why doesn't she swear out a complaint and do the world a favor?"

"Think he'll ever push her far enough?"

"Christ, between his temper and her patience, I'm beginning to think they deserve each other."

"Hey, Wade!" Luke was at the door, looking considerably more cheerful.

"What's up?"

"Lauren's on the phone. She says you're out of charcoal and the store's closed, so she volunteered you to take us all out for pizza."

"Oh, she did, did she? That's very generous of her."

Luke smiled. "That's what I told her. And just to make sure you don't squirm out of it, she and Margie are coming down to pick us up in about five minutes."

"What about Debbie and Lynn Marie?"

"They've been invited over by some other kids in the parade. Besides, Lauren says we'll be back before their bedtime."

"Well, tell her to make it *ten* minutes; I'm buying Ev a drink."

"Tell her yourself; I don't want to get caught in the middle of this."

Everett started to laugh. "Might as well marry her, Wade. She's already spending your money anyway."

"Yeah. Meet you across the street."

Alone on the sidewalk, Everett stepped off the curb. Suddenly, out of the limp night air, a violent gust of wind came up, forcing him to grab his hat to keep it from blowing away. He grumbled at the curious phenomenon, which vanished as quickly as it had come. Then, as he was crossing the street, something in the shadows caught his eye.

It looked like a car—a parked black car.

X

Everett moved slowly down the all-but-deserted street. A Navajo woman walked along the sidewalk, taking little notice of the sheriff. Amos Clements, still standing where his truck had been, stepped off the curb and started to angle across the street toward The Great Western Booze Factory, placing himself between Everett and the parked car.

It was a scene so commonplace that it would have barely registered with a passerby.

As Everett approached the car, he thought he detected a low, steady, purring sound. Was it the smooth idle of a finely tuned engine? He tried to tell himself no, that it was simply an empty parked car, and when he got close enough to pare away the shadows, he'd see that it was green or maroon or . . .

Everett stopped in his tracks. Had the car moved, or was it merely a trick of the imperfect light? He stood there, his muscles tensed, his right hand sliding automatically toward his gun.

He waited—for what, he wasn't sure—but all his instincts told him something was going to happen.

There it was! This time he definitely saw the car inch forward, like a cat taking a single perfect step toward its prey. And in the instant it took him to assimilate the move, its parking lights snapped on, illuminating the chromium death mask of its bumpers and grill in a smoky, amber glow.

"Wade! Wade! Get out here! Quick!"

Wade threw the phone receiver on the table and rushed for the door. What he saw when he got there left him immobilized, his senses focused on a few seconds of time he would remember for the rest of his life.

The car's headlights sprang to life and it leaped forward in a stunning display of acceleration, chewing up the distance in what seemed like a disdainful eclipse of the laws of time and motion.

Before Amos had even a glimmer of what was happening, the car was upon him. But as the awful realization of his death bore down on him, the car nimbly swerved to its left, purposely avoiding him, and Amos managed to propel himself into a dive for the gutter.

The leviathan hurtled on. The sheriff's hand clawed frantically at the strap across his gun, but it was too late.

Everett's scream and the sickening thud of the car against his body sent Wade rushing out the door and into the street. The black machine flashed by him in a savage blur.

A moment later Luke was on the scene, kneeling by the sheriff as Wade scrambled into a patrol car and took off in pursuit.

Everett lay sprawled on the pavement, the spreading flow of blood from his stomach and pelvis a dark, wet stain in the dim light. Luke was only vaguely aware of the small gathering of onlookers who had come from the surrounding buildings. The sole thought that ran through his mind over and over again was that the car had taken three good people in a single day's foraging.

* * *

Wade's car raced along the highway, its siren slicing through the still night, the flashing red lights reflecting on the polished surface of the hood.

He gripped the wheel tightly, his eyes set on the twin dots of the taillights that hung seemingly suspended in the darkness a good hundred yards in front of him.

He pressed the accelerator to the floor and the thin red needle of the speedometer nudged the one-twenty mark, but it did no good; the gap between himself and the receding taillights steadily widened. Then, like two pinpoints of flame being simultaneously extinguished, they went out.

Wade knew the road well; there was no curve ahead, and the lights hadn't faded into the distance. They'd simply disappeared. But how? If the driver had turned them off in an effort to escape, he was a fool. Hitting the soft shoulder at those speeds would make it virtually impossible to retain control of the car. It would almost certainly flip, and the impact was a sure bet to result in explosion.

Wade half expected to see an orange fireball flare in the darkness, and it would have given him grim satisfaction. But all that loomed in front of him on the deserted road was a black-and-white sign announcing the beginning of Daigler County and the end of his jurisdiction.

His foot automatically moved to the brake; then he slammed the accelerator back down.

Fuck the rules, he said to himself as he sped past the sign into Daigler County. He'd be damned if he was going to let some arbitrary line on a map stop him. There was only one road for the next twenty miles, and that car had to be on it somewhere. Sooner or later those taillights were bound to show up again.

Just as Wade was reaching for his mike to radio ahead, a sudden thought flashed through his mind. What if the black car were waiting for him, parked across the road, the maniac driver patiently counting the seconds until the pulverizing, metal-fusing impact?

Wade slammed on his brakes and brought his car to a screeching halt. Jamming the gearshift into park he leapt out, the stench of burning rubber filling his nostrils.

He ran a few steps ahead, gun drawn, eyes straining into the night, every fiber of his being willing the damnable car to take shape before him.

The moonlit landscape lay vacant and taunting, refusing to yield the slightest glimpse of his enemy.

Behind him, the cry of his car's siren seemed only another indication of his impotence.

Holstering his gun, Wade turned and walked back, the still-flashing pursuit lights lending momentary bursts of blood red illumination to his features, his mind already picturing the scene he knew he would have to face when he returned to the station.

The epidemic had arrived, and he had some very real doubts about whether he'd be able to control it.

XI

Everett's body still lay in the street, a blood-soaked sheet shielding it from the crude stares of milling onlookers, the number of whom had increased considerably since the time of the killing. As Wade's car pulled slowly to the curb, they gathered around it, shouting questions in frightened, angry tones.

"Was it the same car that got the Pullbrook girl?"

"How come you're not out there chasing it?"

"Jesus Christ, isn't anybody safe around here anymore? When the sheriff gets it right in front of the goddamn station, seems to me like we're all in deep trouble."

Wade edged the car door open and stepped out.

"How about it?" someone shouted. "You gonna answer us or aren't you?"

"I will when I have something to tell you," Wade said.

"That's it? We're just supposed to walk away and wait to see who's next?"

"Look! Ev was more than my boss; he was my friend, and I want to get the guy that put him under that sheet more than anything else. But standing here arguing with you people isn't going to help me get the job done. You're all alive—be thankful for it, and get off the streets."

Wade shouldered through the tightly knit group and slammed the station door behind him.

Thompson, manning the switchboard, was in the midst of a call. Chas sat at the opposite end of the room facing an old Navajo woman who rested on a bench, her face weathered and lined, her hand-woven shawl clutched tightly around her shoulders. Though she appeared outwardly calm, her eyes reflected the horror of what she had seen.

"Got something?" Wade asked as he walked up to Chas.

"She was a witness. Says she was on the street when it happened."

The woman began to speak in Navajo. When she finished, Chas translated.

"She says she's sorry the sheriff is dead. It was a bad thing."

Wade smiled his thanks, trying to put her at ease. "Ask her if she got a good look at the car."

Chas put the question to her. Her answer was brief and Chas gave a sigh of defeat. "She says it was black. Big and black."

"Does she know what kind?"

The woman listened to Chas, then shook her head no.

"What about the driver?" Wade prodded. "Did she get any kind of a look at the driver? Big, little, dark, light?"

Chas spoke again, obviously trying to convey the importance of the question, but she only shrugged helplessly and spoke a few quick words.

Chas turned to Wade. "It was dark, and it happened fast."

"Yeah, I know what she means. I was a witness too, and a trained one, to boot. But big and black was all I saw. I should have seen more, but I didn't, and I'll be damned if I know why."

"Not even in pursuit?" Chas asked hopefully.

"Are you kidding? I couldn't get within a hundred yards of that bastard. He must have one hell of an engine in that thing."

Thompson walked over to them. "I just checked with Daigler. They're watching, but no sign of him."

"There's one road out there," Wade said. "He couldn't have gone anyplace *but* Daigler County."

"That's what I told them," Thompson said lamely.

"Then tell them again. They've got to sight him sooner or later. He can't just vanish." As he said the words, Wade thought of the disappearing taillights he'd chased down the highway. He was about to mention it, then caught himself. "Check in with Daigler every half hour."

"Right," Thompson said, and he moved back to the switchboard.

The Navajo woman spoke, her voice carrying the inflection of a question.

"She wants to know if she can go," Chas said.

"Yeah, tell her okay; we're not going to get any more out of her than we already have."

Chas relayed the message and the woman stood up. She took a few steps, then turned back to the two men and began to speak in a quick, agitated tone. When she finished, there was a look of unmistakable fear on her face.

"What is it?" Wade asked urgently.

Chas dismissed it with a subtle gesture. "She's an old woman. It's just Indian talk—doesn't really matter."

"Maybe it does; we can't afford to dismiss anything."

Chas looked a little embarrassed. "She says the car

is evil. It could have killed Amos but it didn't, because
he's evil too. She and her family are heading for the
back country tomorrow; the old ones say bad things are
comin' with the wind."

The woman grabbed Wade's arm for a moment, as if
to reinforce her warning. Then she turned and hurried
out the door, leaving an uncomfortable aura behind that
neither of the men could shake.

"Well . . . Chief . . ." Chas finally said, "what do we
do now?"

Wade looked at him and spoke with disarming frank-
ness. "I don't know, Chas. I honestly don't know."

Wade crossed the street, noticing the roadblocks that
had been set up to cordon off the area where Everett
lay, thankful that the deputies who'd been called back
had managed to get the agitated spectators to clear
off. The last thing he wanted was to face another
gauntlet of questions, especially when he didn't have
any answers.

The purple neon script that spelled out The Great
Western Booze Factory flickered in the humid night air.
Inside, the establishment was every bit as garish as its
name implied. Brassieres of the grossest proportions
were draped over rotting deer heads, autographed jock
straps decorated the walls, a gargantuan garter belt
hung from the gilt mirror behind the bar. But, Utah not
being the wettest state in the Union, it was the only
saloon in town, so the owner's questionable tastes had
to be tolerated.

Wade quickly scanned the room and spotted his man.
Hoping he could hold his temper in check, he crossed
to the bar and shouldered in next to Amos, who barely
glanced at him, sullenly enjoying his newly found

celebrity status as a survivor of the car. He held a half-finished drink in his left hand, his right apparently injured in his escape; two or three light abrasions marred the right side of his face.

"Like to ask you a couple of questions if you're up to it," Wade said.

Amos took a pull on his drink and made no answer.

"A good man's lying dead out in the street; I need all the help I can get. You've seen the car twice. *Now* can you give me a better description of it?"

"I saw the gutter, period." Amos spoke the words to the drink in front of him.

"You must at least know whether it was the same car that killed the hitchhiker."

Amos turned his head slowly toward Wade. "Yeah, it was the same car."

"Well, that's a start."

"And a finish, 'cause that's all I know."

"You get hurt bad?"

"Nothin' to speak of."

"That's a shame."

"Listen, Junior, you were chasin' it, so where the hell is it?"

"In Daigler County."

"That wouldn't have stopped your father. County lines didn't mean shit to him. He'd still be out runnin' that fuckin' car into the ground instead of parkin' his fat ass on a bar stool."

Wade flared and backhanded the drink out of Amos' hand just as Marsha, the bartender, walked up. A well-developed blonde in her mid-thirties, she had a not unattractive figure and an extremely tolerant nature; the latter had served her well on more than one occasion, for the group at the Booze Factory was often rowdy.

She casually picked up the overturned glass and

mopped up the spill with a bar cloth, much too experienced to let a little incident like this bother her.

"I'm sorry about Ev," she said to Wade.

"Aren't we all." He looked across at Amos. "Another round for Slim, here. Seems I got a little clumsy. And you can bring me some gin, and don't be stingy."

She turned to make the drinks.

"That could have been me laying out there in the street," Amos said. "But I dove; I moved."

"What's that supposed to mean?"

Marsha set down a large glass filled with ice in front of Wade. Next to it she put an unopened bottle of gin.

"It means just what I said," Amos continued while Wade cracked the seal on the bottle cap and poured a healthy slug of gin into his glass. "The car swerved. I dove. It missed me."

Wade drained his glass, letting the liquor burn its way into his chest. "Didn't want to waste his time with you, huh?"

Marsha set down Amos' fresh drink. He took a pull on it and glared at Wade. "You got yourself a killer to catch, hotshot. I just hope you're up to it."

"That's okay. We've got one big advantage."

"Oh, yeah?"

"If he purposely passed up a guy like you, he must be one dumb sonofabitch." Wade refilled his glass and held it up to Amos. "Your treat." Then he slid off the stool and walked out, carrying his drink with him.

Outside, the scene that greeted him made him take a large swallow of gin. The ambulance had arrived, and Everett's body was being lifted in. Chas, standing close by, reached out at the last minute to touch Everett's limp hand in a final gesture of farewell.

Wade couldn't bring himself to go any closer, and as he stood on the sidewalk in front of the saloon he saw Lauren, Margie, and Luke come out of the station and start across to him.

Lauren was in the lead by a few steps, her face a mixture of sorrow and concern. Behind her, Margie had her arm around Luke's waist. He was visibly upset, moving with the dazed gait of a shell-shocked combatant.

When they reached him, Wade raised his glass in a limp hello.

Lauren cupped his head in her hands and kissed him gently. "I'm sorry," she said. "I'm so terribly sorry."

"I know." He spoke barely above a whisper.

"Is there anything I can do?"

"Mind spending the night with the kids? I'm going to be tied up here."

"Of course."

"You don't think there's any chance he'll come back, do you?" Margie asked.

"Why not? He came back for Ev." Luke's voice was hollow.

"But why?" Lauren said. "Who would do a thing like that? What kind of *monster?* My God, Ev was . . ."

"A good man." Luke finished the sentence for her. "And Susan Pullbrook was a fine young girl. The hitchhiker—just a harmless boy passing through. And Pete Keil, he just wanted to spend some time with his girl."

"Pete?" Margie interrupted.

"He was on a bicycle trip with Suzie," Wade said. "We haven't found him yet."

"Christ, what's happening around here?" Margie tightened her arm around Luke's waist.

"And then there's Amos Clements," Luke said. "Alive and well."

"What are you getting at?" Wade asked.

Luke heaved a deep sigh and shook his head slowly, staring at the ground. "Nothing, I suppose."

Margie shot Wade a worried glance, and he understood.

"Go home and get some sleep, Luke."

Luke looked up at him. "What about tonight?"

"The only thing we can do tonight is wait. I'd rather have you fresh in the morning."

"You're going to need everyone you can get."

"Not if they're all dead on their feet tomorrow."

"Wade's right, honey," Margie urged. "Let's go home."

Luke knew precisely what everyone was concerned about, and he was simply too tired to bother to object.

The unexpected sound of an engine turning over startled them, and then they realized it was only the ambulance pulling away.

They watched it go; then Lauren broke the silence.

"I'll go see to the kids," she said to Wade. "Can I bring you anything?"

"No thanks."

"Take care," Margie said, and she and Luke moved off across the street.

"I'm sorry to put all this on you, Lauren. The kids and everything."

"Don't be silly; you know I love them. You're the one I'm worried about. Are you sure you're going to be okay?"

He smiled and nodded. "No sweat."

"The hell it isn't. If you need anything, just holler."

She gave him a gentle kiss. "You're going to beat this thing, Wade; I just know you are." She squeezed his hand and turned to leave.

"Lauren?"

She looked back over her shoulder.

"Tomorrow, maybe, we'll talk."

"Whenever you're ready," she said, and she walked away into the shadows.

Later that night Margie lay in a restless sleep, living a dream she thought she'd defeated a long time ago. Flames licked at the blackness around her. Sirens lacerated the night. The church was burning, its wooden frame crackling in the heat, its rafters buckling in explosions of orange sparks. She screamed at Luke to come out, but he wanted to die. He wanted to burn with his father's intolerable church, damning them both in a drunken fury.

She awoke with a start, her body covered with a thin patina of sweat, and in those first few seconds of disoriented reality her ears strained to identify a muffled, faraway sound. Was it the rhythmic rise and fall of a revving engine?

She was afraid; her arm moved to Luke's side of the bed, but she was alone. Again, the distant noise ruffled a nameless quadrant of the night, and this time she was sure it was the rumble of an engine.

It was out there somewhere, she thought. Waiting. Watching.

She threw back the covers, and just as she was swinging to a sitting position, she heard another sound— from within the house.

Clicking on the nightstand lamp, she softly padded out of the bedroom and down the short hallway, coming to a stop at the entrance to the kitchen.

Margie stood on the threshold, her eyes peering into the soft darkness, sick at what she was seeing. Then she reached around the corner and flicked on the light.

Luke looked up from the kitchen table, raising his liquor glass in a mocking toast.

"Happy anniversary," he said.

Then he set the glass down with a bang and buried his head in his arms.

Margie rushed over to him, knelt down, and held him tightly, searching desperately for the right words. Then her glance fell on the open Bible in front of him, and on the underlined passage from Peter:

> *Be wary, be vigilant; because your adversary the devil, as a roaring lion, walketh about, seeking whom he may devour.*

XII

At seven forty-five the following morning the front door to the sheriff's station slammed shut behind "Big Dan" Garrett, the mayor of Santa Ynez. He strode directly up to Wade's desk, hauled over a vacant chair, and sat down.

"Big Dan" came by his nickname more than honestly. He stood six-feet-five and weighed in at somewhere around two-forty. He didn't look anything near his true age (forty-three), and he rarely thought twice about using his size and strength to make a point—political or otherwise.

There were those who said his three consecutive terms as mayor were due largely to fear on the part of his opponents, but he was an atypical politician, as uncompromising as he was fair, and most people thought he was just what the town needed. But that particular morning, Wade wasn't exactly relishing a visit from the big man.

"Congratulations," Dan said.

"On what?"

"You're the new sheriff."

"By succession; Ev was my friend."

"Sorry. You know what I meant. But you've inherited yourself one hell of a mess, and as mayor I've got to know what you're doing about it."

"We've got all the surrounding counties on alert, and roadblocks damn near every place a car could go."

"Will that get the job done?"

"You want a straight answer or a comfortable one?"

"You have to ask that, you may not be sheriff for long."

"Okay then. The answer is I just don't know. I chased that guy last night; by all rights, I should've been able to catch him. But I didn't—couldn't even come close. He headed straight into Daigler. They've known what to look for ever since that hitchhiker got it yesterday morning, and they haven't come up with a single solid lead. So you tell me: where the hell is he?"

Dan brought a huge fist crashing down on the desk. "Damnit, Wade, we just can't sit around and wait to be picked off one by one!"

"Do we have any other choice? We start hauling in everyone who drives a black car, the only thing we're gonna accomplish is to make the lawyers wealthy. It's his move, Dan. The only thing we *can* do is wait."

"Meanwhile, we've got ourselves a town full of edgy people. If that bastard gets in here again and kills someone else, this place'll come apart like a shithouse in a tornado."

"You think I don't know that? Look, I'd like to nail the guy so bad I can taste it. But I also know the best thing that could happen to us is if we never see that black car again."

Dan leaned back in his chair and appraised the new sheriff. "You're a realist; so am I. And I hope for both our sakes that that sonofabitch is just as far away from here as he can get. But if anything new turns up, I want you on the horn to me right away. Understand?"

"I understand."

Dan pushed his huge bulk to his feet, then flashed Wade a broad grin. "So long, Sheriff."

Wade watched him go. He'd heard enough about Dan Garrett to know he only backed a man after careful consideration. In this case, Dan didn't have much of a choice, but Wade knew full well that if things got too far out of hand, he'd have a very short tenure as sheriff. And if that happened, the only thing left for him to do would be to resign.

As he sat there, he toyed with the thought of what his life would be like away from the department. It wasn't a pleasant perspective. There were too many people around who still idolized the memory of his father. That would mean a move from Santa Ynez and uprooting Debbie and Lynn Marie, who would both be ashamed that *their* father had failed—with their mother and in his job.

When he'd woken up yesterday morning, he'd been able to see his life stretching out before him with only subtle variations at best. Now, in the space of twenty-four hours, he was suddenly sheriff, and his future was an unknown quantity. And then there was Lauren.

Whenever you're ready, she'd said to him last night. Now he wondered if that time would ever come.

The buzzing of the switchboard brought him back to the present. The men were arriving for morning muster, and he had a day to get through—a day that he prayed would be devoid of any confrontation with the black car.

Several deputies gathered around Wade's desk, the haggard looks on many of their faces testimony to the long hours they'd put in. Wade surveyed the lot: Luke, Fats, Denson, MacGruder, Tattleman, and the others, and began his instructions.

"For those of you just coming on duty, things haven't changed. There's been no definite sighting of the car, and at this stage of the game, there probably won't be. It looks like he got past us somehow and went over the hills, but we'll keep everything going—roadblocks, the works—till I tell you otherwise.

"I know a lot of you have put in some tough hours, and I want to thank every one of you for hanging in there. Whether we catch this guy or not, I know you've all done the best job you could.

"That's it, I guess. Go to it."

The men dispersed, Tattleman, Luke, and a few others going to their desk assignments.

Donna called across from the switchboard. "Wade, we might have something here. Daigler County reports a black vehicle, two-door, unidentified make, going north on Interstate Twelve. They want to know if that sounds like our car."

"They've had the description for twenty-four hours, goddamnit! Tell them to get on it! Right away!"

She turned back to the switchboard and relayed the message.

The front door opened and Dick Mackey, a local funeral director, walked in. Wade waved him over to his desk.

A short, unprepossessing man, Mackey had inherited his business from his uncle, and he had been a reluctant heir at best. Now he was looking uncomfortable in his starched white shirt and black tie.

"Morning, Dick."

"Morning, Wade. Listen, I know you've got your hands full here, but we're on our way over to claim the sheriff's body at the hospital, and he has no next of kin, so I thought maybe you'd be the one . . ." He fidgeted nervously with the knot in his tie.

"Let's have the paper," Wade said.

Mackey thrust a form toward him and Wade scrawled his name on the bottom line.

Reaching to retrieve the paper, the mortician continued his speech, which was obviously rehearsed. "I'm afraid I have no one else to ask about the funeral arrangements."

"He was Methodist," Wade answered. "Give us a couple of days; the guys and I'll take care of the expenses."

"That's very kind. I'll contribute my services, of course, so the costs should be minimal."

"Thanks, Dick. I'll be in touch."

"Have a good day," Mackey said without thinking.

"Yeah, let's hope so."

Mackey was on his way out when Donna called across again.

"Hey, Chief, Daigler County's lost sight of that black two-door. They report no visual contact from any of the checkpoints."

"What the hell, they just saw it, didn't they?"

"What can I say?"

Again he thought of the vanishing taillights he'd chased the night before. "Okay, okay. Tell them to keep looking."

"One more thing," she said.

"Yeah?"

"Miss McDonald, the school principal, called. Wants to know about the parade rehearsal this morning. Can she go ahead?"

"Give her a conditional okay. She won't like it, but tell her it's the best we can do right now."

"Gotcha."

"Tattleman?" The deputy, a heavyset, likable fellow, turned from his desk toward Wade.

"I want to put you on that parade," Wade continued. "Check with McDonald to see what time she wants it scheduled. And if you don't hear otherwise, go ahead with it."

"Right. Just one question."

"Like what?"

"What's a nice guy like me gonna do around all those horses?"

"Fake it." Wade smiled. He got up and crossed the room to Luke's desk.

"How's it going?"

"Okay, I guess. Just a little tired."

"Wasn't much of a night for sleeping, was it?"

Luke immediately wondered if Margie had said anything about his drinking. "It was a rough night for everybody."

"You can say that again."

Wade glanced across to an automatic coffee maker. "Looks like the brew's ready. Can I bring you a cup?"

"Why? Do I look like I need it?"

"Forget it; I was just asking."

"Sorry. Listen, maybe I'm running scared, but I think you're taking a chance with that parade rehearsal. All those kids lined up like that; I hate to think what could happen."

"Makes sense; we might as well be on the safe side." He looked across at Donna and saw that she was on a call. "Do me a favor, Luke. Call McDonald and cancel it. Tell her tomorrow might be a better day."

Wade was just about to tell Tattleman he'd changed his mind when Donna's voice reached him. "Chief, I've got a Mr. Jenkins on the line. Says he's been fishing near Arrigo's Bridge and hooked a . . . well, there's a young man's body in the stream. He guesses maybe twenty years old."

"Oh, God, it's Pete," Luke said, covering his face with his hands.

Wade laid a hand on his shoulder. "That's got to be the Keil boy," he called across to Donna. "Tell Jenkins to stay where he is—I'm on my way."

He was going to say something else to Luke, but thought better of it. Hurrying to his desk, he grabbed his jacket.

"Get an ambulance out there," he told Donna as he passed the switchboard. Then he hesitated, looking back at her, his hand holding the front door half open.

"Something else?" she asked.

"Yeah," he said reluctantly, "put in a call to Dan Garrett and let him know what's happened."

The door banged shut behind him, and he was gone.

A few seconds later, Luke stood up and walked calmly toward the corridor leading to the rear of the station.

Outside, he moved with deliberate steps to his car. Opening the trunk, he lifted the cardboard flooring and withdrew a half pint of liquor in a brown paper bag.

Glancing over his shoulder once, he unscrewed the cap and tilted the welcome bottle to his lips.

XIII

Karl Jenkins sat beside his camper, impatiently sipping hot coffee from a Thermos. When he saw Wade's car pull up, he set down the steaming cup and lumbered over to the sheriff.

A perennial bachelor, Karl was in his early fifties, a squat, stubborn bear of a man who enjoyed life in its basics, and Wade had scarcely had a chance to plant his two feet on the ground before Karl was at him.

"What in holy hell's goin' on around here?"

"Take it easy, Karl."

"You just come with me, and then we'll see who's gonna take it easy."

He trudged across to the stream, picked up the fishing pole that was lying on the ground, and started to reel in his line. The monofilament soon grew taut, angling sharply down into the gently flowing water. Then, the lure's treble hook firmly imbedded in it, a human hand broke the surface, its frozen fingers beckoning in an unearthly welcome.

"All ready to take it easy now, Sheriff?"

Wade walked slowly forward, sloshing into the stream. There beneath the clear, blue-green water, the bloated, wide-eyed corpse of Pete Keil stared up at him, its blonde hair brushed gently by the flowing water, its mouth agape in a soundless cry of terror.

"Nice day for fishin', huh, Sheriff?"

Wade wheeled in a fury. "Jesus Christ, Karl, what do you want from me?"

"An end to the slaughter! A town we can live in again! Is that too much to ask?"

"Maybe it is! Why don't you take over my job and find out?"

Karl threw down his pole and the stiff hand of the corpse sank beneath the rippling surface, glancing off Wade's shoe as it settled to the bottom. The contact sent a streak of nausea shooting through Wade's gut.

Wade closed his eyes for a moment, letting the chill of the current seep into his body and calm him. And as he stood there, Karl's plea for safety still fresh in his mind, he realized that Dan Garrett wasn't the only one he'd have to satisfy if he intended to keep his job.

His legs dragging against the water, Wade stepped onto dry land and made his way back to Karl's camper, where the fisherman was once again sipping on his coffee.

"I could use a cup of that, if you've got any extra," Wade said.

"I suppose I do." Karl got up and went inside the camper, reappearing shortly with a heavy earthenware mug that he thrust out silently to Wade.

"I ain't no waitress," Karl said. "Help yourself."

Wade took the mug and filled it with coffee. He took a cautious sip and almost burned his tongue.

"Got any idea who he is?" Karl asked sullenly.

"The boy? Name's Pete Keil. Seems he was out on a bicycle trip with Susan Pullbrook."

"I'd heard something about her havin' someone with her."

"From who?"

Karl shrugged. "Just around. Late yesterday afternoon. That's when I decided to get me some breathing room, away from the craziness. Guess I didn't pick a very good place, did I?"

"With any luck, this'll be the last of them." Wade disliked the clinical tone of his statement, but hoped he wouldn't be proven wrong.

"That makes four, then?"

Wade nodded and took another sip of coffee.

"That sumbitch must be crazy, runnin' people down like that."

"I sure wouldn't like to think he was sane and doing it for . . . for what?"

"And where the hell did he come from? Just showed up yesterday and started killin' people. And why us? It's almost like he had some kind of private war against us. Shit, four people dead; three of 'em I never heard a bad word against. And that hitchhiker probably never did anybody any harm either. I been through my share in my time, but I'm gonna tell you somethin'—I'm scared. Yes sir. I never thought I'd live to see anything like this, and now that I'm in it, it scares the piss outta me."

Wade was about to answer when the sound of an approaching engine leaped into the stillness. For an instant of panic, the two men could do nothing but focus on the bend in the road; then the lumbering shape of the ambulance came into view and each felt secretly ashamed at his fear.

Wally was the first out, and he walked over to Wade with grim resignation. "This the one we couldn't find yesterday?"

"Right."

Wally shook his head sadly. "Well, point me in the right direction."

"You'll find him at the end of my fishing line," Karl said.

"Terrific. You know, they keep telling me I'm part of the medical profession, but between yesterday and to-day I'm beginning to feel like a garbage collector."

"Let's hope this is the end of it," Wade said.

"It sure as hell better be, or I might as well transfer to the coroner's office." He turned to Joe, who was waiting with the lightweight litter. "Come on, let's get this over with."

The two attendants moved off toward the stream, leaving Karl and Wade standing alone.

"Those boys must have been through a lot," Karl said.

"Haven't we all. Look, I've got some calls to make." Wade glanced at his watch. "Roadblock reliefs should be in by now."

"Closin' the barn door a little late, aren't you?"

"That depends, Karl."

"On what?"

"On whether you want that black car locked in, or locked out."

As Wade walked away, a disquieting notion slipped into his mind: for the first time since it had all begun, he'd talked about The Car without thinking about its driver, and for a man who liked his life bounded by neat, square corners, it bothered him more than a little bit.

XIV

After confirming the roadblock positions—Ray Mott at the desert side of town, Fats and Ashbury at the interstate highway, Metcalf and Berry at the west boundary of town—Wade tried to tell himself the area was secure. Then the radio snapped to life.

"Station to zero-one . . . station to zero-one. Are you there?"

He grabbed the mike and pressed the talk-back button, praying that The Car hadn't struck again. "This is zero-one, Donna. What's up?"

"I've got a message for you from Mayor Garrett."

Wade sighed in semi-relief. "I'll bet you do. Let's hear it."

"He wants you to stop in and see him this morning. He says don't bother to make an appointment; he'll be waiting."

"Suddenly I'm an important man. Tell him I'll be there, but there's something I have to get out of the way first."

"Right, Chief. See you when you get here."

"One more thing. I want you to put a call through to the manager of the Zion National Bank. Tell him I'm on my way over to see Alice Keil, and tell him why."

"It was her son, then?"

"I'm afraid so, but we'll need her for the I.D."

"That's lousy."

"You're not telling me anything I don't already know, kid. See you later."

Wade slipped the mike back into its bracket and started his car. As he jostled along the canyon road, he thought ahead to the two people on his schedule: a hysterical mother and an angry mayor. He tried to decide which of the two would be the more difficult to face and came to the quick conclusion that it was a god-forsaken toss-up.

The employees' lounge at the bank was empty, and Wade had been assured it would be kept that way for the duration of his uncomfortable meeting with Alice Keil.

It was a cheerful room, carpeted in a multitone shag of browns, rusts, and oranges. A service counter lined the rear wall, complete with a double stainless steel sink, two portable microwave ovens, a refrigerator, and—for those employees who didn't adhere to the strict Mormon code—an automatic coffee maker. On a flanking wall stood two vending machines, one for soft drinks and another that offered an array of snacks—crackers and cheese, candy bars, peanuts. The remainder of the wall space was dotted with book shelves and a colorful collection of oil paintings.

There were several seating arrangements grouped about the room, and Wade purposely chose a right-angle combination of two large, vinyl-covered armchairs facing a hexagonal cocktail table. Here they would be just a few feet from the only entrance to the room; thus, Wade would be able to get out easily in the event he needed any assistance. He still remembered the day his father had collected three stitches over his left eye from a hysterical woman, and that was one tradition he'd just as soon not continue.

Wade sat and waited, tense and uncomfortable, the vinyl crackling every time he shifted his position. Then the door opened and Alice was ushered in by Miss Wallace, the operations officer, who discreetly withdrew without saying a word, leaving the two of them alone.

Wade stood up. He was prepared for many things, but none of them was quite the reaction that he got from Alice.

"You were here yesterday, with Luke, weren't you?" she asked calmly.

"Yes, that's right. I'm sorry to have to put you through this, Mrs. Keil."

"Through what?"

Damn, Wade thought, *nobody had the guts to tell her.* Still, she certainly must know the reason behind his visit.

"We found your son this morning," he said gently. "We need you to come to the hospital and make a positive identification."

He waited for a reaction but she just stood there, her eyes blinking every few seconds, and he thought she'd gone into shock. Then she finally spoke.

"That'll mean time off from work; I don't think Miss Wallace will like that. We're short one girl today as it is."

The tone of her answer caught Wade off balance. "Oh, well, I'm sure she'll understand, and we've already spoken to the manager about it."

Alice shrugged her indifference. "If you insist."

"Thank you. We'll make it as quick as possible. My car is outside. Do you have a purse or anything you'd like to bring?"

"Just a moment," she said, and she walked to a

closet and opened it to reveal a grid of sturdy lockers not unlike those found at bus stations and airports. Deftly, she maneuvered the combination on one and removed her purse; then she closed the locker carefully and shut the closet door.

"They think of everything here at the bank. They're really very good to us."

"I'm sure they are," Wade answered. "Shall we go?"

"If you really think we have to," she said. She left the lounge with remarkable composure.

All during the ride to the hospital, Wade expected the dam to break. Alice sat in the back seat and he could feel her eyes on him, but she said nothing. He realized that she probably held him personally responsible for the agony she was about to endure, and he kept telling himself that it was all part of the job—a job that had fit his father so well, a job that had always seemed to Wade a comfortable possibility somewhere in his future. Except now that the future was here, he found it binding and deeply troublesome.

He turned into the hospital parking lot and parked in an Official Vehicle zone near the emergency entrance. When he held the rear door of the patrol car open for Alice she got out steadily, ignoring the offer of his hand.

The pneumatic doors hissed open before them, and they were confronted with five rows of folding chairs holding scattered patients awaiting treatment.

"If you'll wait a moment, I'll see where we have to go," he said to Alice, and he walked quickly up to the admitting window.

"Can I help you?" The young nurse had a warm smile, and Wade was grateful for a kind face.

"I have the mother of Peter Keil here to identify the body; it was brought in a short while ago."

"I see." The mention of death was obviously not unfamiliar to her, and Wade wished he could handle it as easily.

"Take the hallway on your right to the elevator. All the way down to the second basement. You'll see signs when you get there. I'll call ahead and let them know you're coming."

"Thanks."

Alice was waiting patiently where he'd left her, and she followed him silently down the corridor to the elevator. The metal doors slid open as soon as he touched the call button; then he pressed the button marked B2 and they began their descent.

The nurse had been right about there being signs, because the first thing they saw when the elevator doors opened was the word MORGUE stenciled in black paint on a cement block wall and a red arrow directing them to their left. They'd only gone a short distance when a middle-aged man came down the hall toward them. He had thinning hair and wore a white lab coat that flapped about his legs as he walked. A blue plastic badge pinned to the coat identified him as Dr. Stanford.

"Good morning," Stanford said to Wade. "I assume you're here about the I.D. on the dead boy."

He winced at the doctor's bluntness. "That's right; this is Mrs. Keil."

"Follow me, then," Stanford said, and he led them briskly down the corridor and through a door marked STAFF ONLY. Inside, they were immediately assailed by the strong smell of disinfectant.

The doctor walked quickly across the large, white-tiled room. "D-twelve," he snapped at a young assistant who preceded him to a wall of roll-out, refrigerated cubicles.

As Wade and Alice gathered around, Stanford spoke to her directly for the first time.

"You should be aware, Mrs. Keil, that the body was in the water for some twenty-four hours before it was recovered. That can make for a rather shocking appearance."

Then he signaled the attendant, who rolled out the cubicle on its silent track and lifted the sheet that covered the body.

"Is this your son, Mrs. Keil?" Wade heard himself asking.

The eyes had been mercifully closed, the mouth forced shut to stifle the soundless scream, but the face was nevertheless hideous in its lopsided, puffy construction.

"No, that's not him," Alice said firmly, and the sentence took a moment to register with Wade.

"Are you certain?" Stanford asked.

"Of course I'm certain. That's not my boy; Pete's up in Ogden on a job interview. I expect him back any day now."

"But Mrs. Keil," Wade said softly, "he never showed up in Ogden. I told you that yesterday. Remember?"

Alice looked at him with a steady gaze. "And I told you you were a liar. Do you remember that?"

"We have his personal effects, Mrs. Keil," Stanford said, his tone finally a little less clinical. "There are articles that identify him as Peter Keil."

"I don't know anything about that," she said.

"Please, Alice." Wade used her first name in a final attempt at contact. "I know this is very hard for you, but you have to accept the truth. Pete was on a bicycle trip with Susan Pullbrook. They were killed by a car, just like that hitchhiker yesterday morning and Everett last night in front of the station. They're all dead, Alice. All killed by the same car."

It was only then that she began to tremble slightly, as if in a rage at what she was hearing.

"I don't know what you're talking about," she said, struggling to keep her voice under control. "Nobody's dead. Nobody at all. And there's no car. Everything's just like it always was. Now can I get back to work? I don't want to miss too much time, if you don't mind. They need me."

The attendant dropped the sheet and slid the cubicle back into place.

"Do you have a physician, Mrs. Keil?" Stanford asked.

"Doctors couldn't save my husband. What do I need them for?"

"Why don't you let me give you something to calm your nerves? Then perhaps you'll realize what's been happening."

"Nothing's happening! Do you hear me? Nothing!" She hurled the words at the three men as if to batter down their ignorance.

"Mrs. Keil, listen to me." Stanford tried to sound reasonable, but came across patronizing. "I can't do anything for you without your consent, but I strongly recommend that you see a doctor. Painful as it may be, your son is dead, and the quicker you realize that, the further along you'll be on the road to recovery."

"I won't even dignify that with an answer." Then she turned to Wade. "Are you going to take me back to work or aren't you?"

He looked to Stanford for help but received only a cold stare in return.

"Come on," Wade said to Alice. "Let's go."

XV

Alice kept up a pitiful stream of conversation all during the ride back to the bank, assuring Wade that her son had an excellent chance of getting the job in Ogden. And even though she didn't know what it might entail, she was certain that Pete would be well suited for it since he was such a good, conscientious boy. She even went so far as to suggest that once Pete got himself firmly established she might just move up to Ogden herself.

"Why shouldn't I?" she asked as he pulled to the curb. And the ironic truth of her parting words had only intensified the knot in Wade's stomach. "After all, Sheriff, what would keep me here if my son wasn't with me? He's all I live for now that Merle's gone. Yes sir, a move to Ogden might do a world of good for both of us."

Wade could only nod wordlessly and hope that his smile conveyed reassurance instead of the deep sadness he felt. Then, easing out into traffic, he forced himself to concentrate on the next item on his agenda: his meeting with Dan Garrett.

As he drove he tried to play devil's advocate, taking Garrett's position and attempting to second-guess the mayor's point of view. But it soon became apparent that their positions were virtually interchangeable. They were both dealing with the same set of facts: four people killed, almost certainly by the same maniac in the same black car. It was up to Wade to make sure the death list stopped where it was; stopping The Car itself was almost irrelevant at this point. If it were simply never to return, everyone would breathe a collective sigh of relief. The important thing was to make the people of Santa Ynez feel secure enough to carry on their daily routines without fear of violence. That was the bottom line, the responsibility that both he and Dan Garrett shared, with one vital exception—Dan Garrett could fire Wade, and he wouldn't hesitate to do so if he felt it were in the best interests of the town.

Wade pulled up at City Hall, got out, and stepped into the air-conditioned, marble-floored lobby of the two-story structure. It had been built only two years before to replace the inadequate, uncomfortable building that had served as the old City Hall for thirty-seven years.

An eight-by-twelve mural rendered in mosaic tiles and semi-precious stones depicted the founding of Santa Ynez, but Wade took little notice as he walked across to the main switchboard. There, a middle-aged woman was taking advantage of a lull in calls to catch up on a paperback Gothic novel.

"Excuse me," Wade said. "I'm looking for the mayor's office."

"Second floor, all the way down on your left." She didn't even look up from her book.

"Thanks." Then, as he began to climb the staircase that began just a few feet from the switchboard, the woman's voice called out to him.

"Talking to the mayor sure isn't going to help you catch that car."

Wade turned on the stairs to look at the woman. Her book was down now, and though he hadn't the slightest idea who she was, she looked at him with an open hostility he'd rarely encountered in any of the citizens of Santa Ynez. Fighting an impulse to answer her back, he continued up the stairs, feeling her angry stare follow him all the way.

The mayor's office was exactly where she had told him it was, and as he stepped into the reception area, his feet sank into the softness of luxuriously padded carpeting. A young secretary—an attractive, smartly dressed redhead—immediately welcomed him.

"Good morning, Sheriff. Mayor Garrett is expecting you; I'll show you in."

He didn't have time to decide whether this prompt admittance was a good or bad sign, because in a few seconds an ornately carved oak door had been pushed open and Wade was looking across a vast expanse of office at "Big Dan" Garrett.

"Come on in, Wade, and pull up a chair."

The floor seemed like a rippling acre of gently sculptured cream, and Wade settled into a kid-soft leather armchair across from the mayor's massive desk as the office door closed softly behind him.

"Glad you could make it," Dan said.

"I don't recall having been given a choice."

"Good, then we can dispense with the public-servant crap and get down to business. I assume by now you have verification on the body near Arrigo's Bridge?"

"It's the Keil boy, all right."

"Then this is nothing new; when you found the Pullbrook girl it was just a matter of time until you found her boyfriend."

"I suppose."

Dan leaned across his desk. "Don't ever suppose anything. People like to think the sheriff is in complete control at all times."

"If you don't think I am, you can have my resignation any time you want it."

The mayor raised a beefy hand in supplication. "Take it easy. Just a little friendly advice, that's all. If the day ever comes when I want your resignation I won't have to ask you twice for it, believe me."

"Fine," Wade said. "Just so we understand each other."

Dan settled back into his chair. "As soon as your dispatch girl called me with the news about the body, I conducted an informal telephone poll of the town council. If it did nothing else, it made my day to get two of the lazy bastards out of bed."

"And what did they have to say besides good morning?"

"They're beginning to feel the pressure. Nothing obvious, of course. Just a few well-placed remarks by some of the more influential businessmen in town. That's usually the way it starts."

"Sounds like those businessmen are big on hedging their bets."

"For now. But if they begin to feel the pinch in their bank accounts you can be sure they won't mince any words."

"In the meantime all I have to do is go out and catch The Car, right? Well, I've got news for them: we can't catch a car we can't see."

"And I've got news for you: they don't give a shit about The Car, and neither does the council. All they want is a guarantee that it's not going to come back and roll over somebody else."

"That's all, huh? They sound like a real reasonable group."

"That's why they're the councilmen." Dan grinned.

"What the hell do they expect me to do? Put a sign

up at the city limits asking the guy please not to come back? Jesus Christ, Dan, I've got four dead people on my hands and they're talking about guarantees!"

"It's a damn good thing you don't have to run for office. You'd never last two weeks in a campaign."

"I can only react to what I see and hear; I'm not a mind reader."

"Then let me help you out. They're willing to wait and see what happens—for a little while. This may surprise you, but they like the idea of your being sheriff. You're young, you've got a good record with the department, and most of the guys remember the last few years your father was alive. I don't have to tell you the weight his memory carries around here."

"Yeah." Wade felt somehow resentful at the mention of his father. "So what do you suggest I do?"

"I called you here to let you know how things stand, not to tell you how to do your job. I'm saying that because I happen to have confidence in you."

"And if it turns out that you're wrong?"

"Then, my friend, they'll have us both by the balls, because I'll be the one who has to name a new sheriff. And just between you and me, I'm not sure there's anyone else who can handle the job. Not under these circumstances, anyway. So do me a favor. Don't put either of us in a position where we have to find out."

Wade took a few moments to digest the conversation, then stood up. "Well, as somebody once said, you've made yourself perfectly clear."

"I still want to be kept informed if anything breaks."

"If it's all the same to you, the next time I talk to you I'll be asking for a raise."

"Get out of here." Dan smiled. "I've got work to do."

* * *

The switchboard operator in the lobby was busy with a call when Wade passed her on his way out. But as he stepped into the morning sun, he realized why he'd been angry at her remark about talking to the mayor.

He'd been angry because she was right.

XVI

Deputy Sheriff Tattleman was pleased with himself. When Miss McDonald, the school principal, had told him that she'd arranged for the parade practice to be held at the racetrack on the outskirts of town, he'd known exactly where he was going to position himself in order to have a clear view not only of the rehearsal but of the surrounding countryside as well.

Hand over hand, he climbed the iron rungs of the ladder that led to the judges' tower across from the empty grandstand, and as he set foot on the shaded, five-by-five platform he was more satisfied than ever that he'd chosen the perfect spot from which to observe the goings-on.

Slowly, methodically, he began a sweep of the area. The track itself was a moderately large affair, running east to west and used mainly for local fairs and exhibitions. The straightaways were bordered by sloping banks that led to low sandstone cliffs feeding into vast, desert-like plains. To the west of the track was an old cemetery, no longer in use; the surrounding countryside was almost a moonscape, with huge mesas dotting the horizon.

Turning his attention to the people below him, he set the scene firmly in his mind. At the west end of the north straightaway three wranglers were mounted on horseback, keeping a watchful eye on a restless group of some thirty horses gathered behind the school band. Standing with the horses were Margie Johnson and a few other teachers, along with the children who had been selected to be cowboys and cowgirls. Among the milling, anxious participants were Debbie and Lynn Marie Parent and young Jimmy Clements, the last of whom was relishing one of the few happy moments in his otherwise hard young life. The children were dressed in casual street clothes, but they also wore bits and pieces of their costumes in order to promote at least a semblance of the feeling of the actual day of the parade.

Gradually, order settled over the chaos. The band lined up in formation, braided hats on their heads, and each of the cowboys and cowgirls was given a horse. They stood excitedly beside their mounts, reins in hand.

"We're going to walk them through this time, kids," Margie said. "And remember, horses are like people in many ways. They tend to be a little shy of strangers until they get to know them better, so hold the reins gently but firmly. The second time around you can mount up. You should be used to each other by then."

Lauren, standing at the head of the band, surveyed the ranks and decided it was time to begin.

"Okay, Sherry," she called to the lead majorette, "let's get it going."

The nervous young girl gave a downbeat with her baton, there was a snappy drum-roll, and the band lurched forward behind her. She strutted, stepping high, her baton twirling graceful patterns in the air.

Miss McDonald stood on the infield, her head bobbing metronomically in time with the music of the approaching band. Even though the rest of the school was in session, Lauren had fully expected her to be there, for the principal was constantly in attendance at everything from lunch-hour revelry to football practice, swaggering about the grounds like a marine drill sergeant. All she needed to complete the image, Lauren thought, was a pair of calf-high boots and a riding crop. But Lauren paid her little attention on any of these occasions, for she'd very quickly come to the conclusion that Miss McDonald felt insecure sitting behind a desk in an office, and had to oversee events such as this in order to reinforce her feeling of self-importance. It made her feel good to be surrounded by people over whom she had authority—but since most of the teachers and even a fair number of the students recognized that fact, her frequent appearances only served to make her a subject of pity and ridicule.

A few feet away on the infield, a group of mothers stood watching the rehearsal, the pride on their faces diluted by the anxiety they all felt after the previous day's events.

Bertha Clements was among them, a clumsy attempt at makeup only making her bruises look worse.

"God, this makes me nervous," one of the mothers said. "I just don't understand why she went through with it, do you?"

"I asked her," another replied, "and all she said was that the children wouldn't understand a cancellation."

"That's a pretty lame excuse, if you ask me. These children are her responsibility. I had half a mind to keep Bobby home this morning, but it wasn't worth the tantrum I knew he'd throw."

"I suppose that's the way Miss McDonald feels," another added.

"But she gets *paid* to put up with the children; we don't."

"Let's just hope she doesn't stretch it out too long."

"Are you kidding? She loves every minute of it.

She'll probably make them do it three or four times."

"Everett's dead," Bertha suddenly said, raising her usually timid voice above the din of the passing band. "Why are they doing this when Everett's dead?"

The other women would have liked to pretend they hadn't heard the remark, but they were all standing quite close together, so that was impossible. As it was, the words hung there, demanding a reply, and it was only the sound of Lauren's agitated voice that broke the embarrassing lull.

"Bobby, you're slow! Slow! Gregg, you too! Come on, *tempo, everybody! Tempo!*" She walked backward alongside the band, trying to take stock of the different sections, to pinpoint who was playing too fast or too slow. It was a difficult, nerve-wracking assignment, but she was determined to mold the self-conscious children into a cohesive unit.

On the ground, everybody was a jumble of missed beats and increasingly nervous horses, so no one noticed that Deputy Tattleman was squinting into the sunlight from his position in the judges' tower, trying to decide whether the hazy dot of light and dust at the far end of the plain was a moving object or merely a trick of the atmosphere.

The band was passing almost immediately beneath him, temporarily distracting his concentration, and when he glanced back, the dot had grown considerably. He was sure now that it was moving. Rapidly. Heading directly for the racetrack.

A light breeze suddenly flared, flapping the sheet music on the clips of the band instruments. Lauren's voice droned on in the background.

Tattleman didn't want to be responsible for a needless panic. His hands gripped the railing on the judges' tower as he watched the spot on the plain, counting off the precious seconds, praying that the gathering cloud would alter its course.

Another gust of wind flurried, harder than the first, pricking the horses' ears and causing a few of them to stop and sniff the wind for danger. The wranglers quickly moved in and got them going, but the wind gusted again, this time sending music and hats flying; the children broke ranks to give chase, the rousing march dwindling down to the persistent beat of the bass drum.

In the tower, Tattleman drew in a sharp breath at the form that was beginning to take shape in the fast-approaching cloud. He couldn't believe what he was seeing—the sun glinting off flashes of black paint and dust-muted chrome. It was The Car.

The wind whipped across the racetrack with vicious force, plastering the sleeves of Tattleman's shirt to his arms, swirling sand and dirt everywhere. Random voices were raised in shouts of anger and fear, the nervous whinnying of the horses lending a shrill backdrop to the increasing pandemonium.

Then it came, borne on the rushing air like a demented cry of vengeance: the sound of a high-powered engine.

For a suspended instant there was an unnatural calm as that telegraphed warning told them what was coming. Tattleman opened his mouth to plead for order, but it was too late. People rushed in all directions. Mothers searched frantically for their children. Band instruments clattered to the ground. A wild dash was made toward cars parked at the east and west ends of the track.

"No!" Lauren screamed. "Don't go to your cars! Stay on the track between the fences! Don't try to leave!"

Crazed horses added to the panic; they pulled away from stunned children and galloped across the infield, reins dragging dangerously on the ground, the three overwhelmed wranglers riding hard in pursuit.

Tattleman climbed quickly down from the tower, descending into the maelstrom of blind frenzy and trying to fight his way through the crisscrossing bodies to his patrol car. Suddenly, in the midst of his dodging, twisting efforts, two horses rushed by. He felt the glancing blow of the first animal; it knocked him off balance and sent him stumbling hard to the ground, his breath whistling out through his clenched teeth. He remembered telling himself that he had to get up as quickly as possible. Then his world came apart as the hooves of the second horse pounded across his prone body.

At the east end of the track, a group of panting, terrified mothers and children raced toward their parked cars. Just when their goal was almost within reach, the perimeter fence of the track exploded in a shower of splintered wood and the black machine careened onto the track. A second later the crowd of nearly hysterical people was rushing for the safety of the grandstand, children clinging hard to the sweaty grips of their parents' hands, knowing that if they fell they would surely be trampled by the fleeing mob.

For a moment it looked as if The Car were going to follow them right into the stands, but it swooped around behind the aging structure, heading toward the west end of the track and more vulnerable prey.

On the infield, Lauren and Margie were still trying to shout some sense into the bewildered, frightened mass of people. But no one would listen. And even if they had, it would have done them no good. Because, emerging from behind some stalls adjacent to the grandstand, The Car crashed through the infield fence and landed, engine snarling, on the infield.

The next instant it was moving, tires clawing the dirt for traction. The people fled in a mad stampede, not caring who they grabbed or pushed or cut in front of in an effort to gain an extra step on the charging beast. The throb of its engine was a hellish death knell in their ears. But when Lauren glanced over her shoulder she realized it was toying with them, herding them like so many cattle, prolonging their impending slaughter for the exquisite thrill of the chase.

Across the track, the harried wranglers saw what was happening and galloped off toward The Car, hoping to distract it and give the people one last chance at survival.

Their horses pounded across the turf, overtaking the lithe, low-slung mass of The Car and cutting between it and its intended victims.

In a life-and-death ballet the riders made sweep after sweep at the menacing presence, each time coming closer to its sleek black body. Then, cutting a vicious arc on the infield, it turned toward the wranglers, spooking one of the horses. It reared and threw its rider hard to the ground; the base of the wrangler's skull received the force of the impact and he was left unconscious.

Bertha and Jimmy, straggling at the edge of the fleeing crowd, suddenly found themselves cut off by the quickly maneuvering Car.

Like helpless animals they stood paralyzed with fear. The marauding demon was revving its engine, preparing for the attack, when the remaining two wranglers broke between it and its prey, commanding Jimmy and Bertha to run.

In a frenzy of anger The Car spun around after the wranglers, the massive curve of a rear fender striking Jimmy and flinging the boy to the ground. The snap of his right arm left him screaming in pain.

Bertha rushed to her fallen child, scooped him up, and ran toward the near side of the track, following the others—and not knowing whether she was heading for safety or destruction.

The Car sped after the wranglers, a mad, roaring predator bearing down on the crazed horses. One by one they threw their riders, the first man scrambling quickly away, the second landing with a twisting, sideways movement against the trunk deck and then sliding to the ground, his cracked ribs and torn cartilage rendering his once agile body a painful collection of muscle and bone.

Spilling out of the west end of the track, the people instinctively made for the only shelter at hand: the cemetery surrounded by a spiked, iron fence.

Like a scattered column of ants they poured into their sanctuary. Its open gates were flanked by two time-worn stone pillars.

The Car thundered after them, an enraged mass of hurtling steel and chrome heading straight for the cemetery gates. And then, without the slightest provocation, it came to a screeching, rubber-peeling halt in front of the two pillars.

It sat there, growling its challenge, the steady idle of its engine the obscene pant of a frustrated killer.

XVII

Mothers, teachers, and children took refuge behind the tombstones and overgrown shrubbery of the cemetery. Lauren, Margie, Debbie, and Lynn Marie dove for cover behind a large tree, all four gasping to catch their breath. The scattered cries of frightened children ricocheted in the background. Tears ran down Debbie's face and Margie held her head in her lap, gently stroking her soft brown hair.

"We're okay now, honey. We're safe in here," she crooned. "Everything's going to be all right."

Lauren had her arm around Lynn Marie; the trembling child's body was vibrating with fear.

"Why did it stop?" Lynn Marie finally asked. "Why didn't it chase us in?"

Lauren and Margie looked at each other, but neither had the answer.

"I don't know," Lauren said. "Maybe . . . maybe it's afraid."

"Of dead people?" Debbie sobbed.

Margie looked around at the maze of old-fashioned tombstones and monuments that jutted into the air.

"There's no *way*, he could run that thing through here."

From where they were hiding they had a good view

of the front gate. The Car held its position, the engine revving angrily, as if challenging the people to come out. But as vicious as it sounded, it still wasn't moving.

"Doesn't look like he's going to leave, does it?" Lauren said. "We've got to get some help."

"How?" Margie couldn't hide the skepticism in her reply.

"It'd take both of us," Lauren said hesitantly.

"Doing what?"

"Well, if one of us could distract his attention, the other might have time to go over the fence, get to Tattleman's car, and call in."

Margie thought for a moment, continuing to stroke Debbie's hair.

"I suppose," she finally said, "I could get over the fence near the back of the cemetery."

"Oh, no," Lauren's voice was firm. "It was my idea; I'm the one who sees if it works."

"Don't," Lynn Marie said unconsciously. "I mean, don't either of you go. Let somebody else do it. We love you." The last words were directed at Lauren, and she hugged the little girl hard.

"I love you, too. Both of you. But don't worry; I'll be okay. I promise."

"Especially since you're going to be staying here and making faces at that dude in the car," Margie told Lauren.

"Give me one good reason."

"I'll give you three. Number one, I can outrun you in my sleep and you know it. Two, you probably never climbed a fence in your life. And three, you better hurry up and let me do it before I change my mind. This hero stuff wears thin pretty fast."

Lauren wished she'd never mentioned the idea.

"You sure?" she asked Margie.

"Only about the last one, so let's hurry up and get going."

"Okay. I guarantee you I'll keep that car here, no matter what I have to do."

"And we'll help you," Debbie said.

"No you won't. You'll both stay right here and take care of each other. Do you understand that?"

"You know," Lynn Marie said to Lauren, "for a neat teacher, every now and then you say something pretty dumb."

"I'm allowed that twice a year. But remember, this is still school time, so you two do exactly as I say."

Without waiting for a reply, Lauren stepped from behind the tree and walked out to the middle of a dirt path that put her in plain view of The Car. Hands on her hips, she confronted the black behemoth.

"Hey, you!" she yelled.

The engine roared its reply.

"What's that? I can't hear you."

The engine revved to a pounding pitch, then subsided to a threatening idle.

Lauren picked up a big stick and took a few cautious steps forward, her eyes fixed on the amber windshield that slanted up to the squat, lowered roofline. The nose of the long, sculptured hood, its vertical grill separating two single, staring headlights, was pointed directly at her. This was the first sustained look she'd had at The Car, and she couldn't help wondering whether her reactions would be quick enough if the powerful mass of its several thousand pounds suddenly charged her.

"Come on!" she taunted. "Why don't you get out of that ugly car? I want to see what you look like! I really want to see what a creep like you *looks like!*"

The Car slipped into gear and rolled backward, as if

getting ready to spring. Lauren jumped back at the quick movement, making sure there was a nearby tombstone she could reach if she had to. But she knew that if her plan were to have any chance of success, she'd have to keep the driver's attention.

"I said get out, not back up, stupid! Not very bright, are you?"

The Car shifted gears, wheeled around in a tight three-hundred-sixty-degree circle, and charged for the front gate, stopping again just short of the entrance.

Timing her move well, Margie had used the opportunity to start her race across the cemetery. Every few yards she dropped behind a tombstone so as not to present a continuous field of movement that the driver of The Car might spot.

"Come on! Get out of your big bad car and let me see you! You lunatic sonofabitch!"

The engine revved five or six times in frustrated fury.

"Well, let's go! Crawl on out, slime, unless you're chicken!"

Behind the tree, Debbie and Lynn Marie looked at each other in wide-eyed glee. Then they decided to reinforce Lauren's challenge by clucking loudly like chickens. Almost immediately the other children picked it up, hooting and blowing on band instruments as well, giving Margie a chance to make several short sprints toward a far section of the iron fence.

"*Chicken! Chicken! Chicken!*" Lauren screamed. "I've got your story now. As long as you're in the car, you're big and bad! Well, I've got news for you, little boy, I think I could kick your ass if you got out from behind that wheel! So come on! Give me a chance!"

She hurled her stick at The Car. It landed squarely against the windshield and the engine wailed in protest.

Margie reached the fence, grabbed a crossbar, and started to pull herself up.

"CHICKENSHIT!" Lauren screamed. "NO GOOD, SCUM-OF-THE-EARTH, SONOFABITCHING CHICKENSHIT! COME OUT AND DO SOMETHING ABOUT IT!"

Margie struggled to the top of the fence, swinging a leg over the dangerous spikes.

Without warning, The Car charged one of the stone pillars, sending chunks of masonry falling to the ground. Lauren took cover behind a tombstone, her eyes never leaving the enraged beast. It retreated and charged the pillar again, this time knocking it at a lopsided angle. But the display of anger and strength wasn't what held Lauren fascinated. It was the unreal fact that The Car bore not the slightest evidence of its contest: the paint was unmarked, the lines of the fender and grill completely preserved, and the headlight that by all odds should have been shattered by the first blow remained totally intact.

Across the cemetery, Margie lowered herself down the other side of the fence, dropping the last few feet to the ground.

At that precise moment, as if sensing her escape, The Car wheeled to its right and raced to the corner of the cemetery, turning right again and heading for the area where Margie had gone over the fence.

Under cover of some bushes between the cemetery and the racetrack, Margie dove for safety, her body a throbbing mass of tension as the beast thundered by. It turned another corner, continuing its circumnavigation of the cemetery, and she sprinted for the track, heading directly for Tattleman's car, which was parked near the grandstand.

Seconds later, the black Car was back at the gate,

seemingly satisfied that its quarry was still neatly caged in.

Praying that Margie was safe, Lauren walked back out onto the dirt path, knowing that if she didn't continue her tirade the driver would certainly realize that something was wrong.

"Well, little one, enjoy your run around the block? I'll bet you did. Makes you feel important racing around like that, doesn't it? I still want to see you, you know. I still say I can whip your ass if you'll just get out of that kiddie car."

This time she got no reaction, and it worried her.

On the track, Margie reached Tattleman's car and saw him crawling toward it from the opposite direction, painfully nursing a broken leg.

She rushed over to him and knelt down. His face was dripping perspiration.

"I want to call for help," she said through short gulps of air. "How do I use the radio?"

"Push . . ." His voice was weak and she was afraid he was going to pass out on her. She damned herself for never having had Luke show her how to use the radio.

"Please, you've got to tell me!"

"Push the button on the mike and talk. Let up and they'll answer you."

She ran back to the patrol car, threw open the door, and grabbed the mike.

"Hello, hello!" she called frantically. "Somebody, hello!"

No reply came, and then she remembered to let up on the talkback button.

"Who is this? I repeat, who is making this call? Identify yourself." Donna's voice became the most beautiful sound Margie had ever heard.

She pressed the button and almost screamed into the mike.

"This is Margie Johnson! The Car has the school band and all of us trapped in the old cemetery above the racetrack. Please, for God's sake, get somebody out here!"

XVIII

Wade was cruising the north end of town when Margie's distress call came over the radio. He lunged for the mike and immediately cut in on the conversation.

"Donna, this is Wade. I've heard and I'm on my way. Get every free car out to that cemetery! Fast! *And where the hell is Luke?* He was supposed to cancel that rehearsal!"

"Nobody's here, Chief. They all took off when they heard Margie."

"All right. Everybody on roadblocks is to hold their position. I'm accepting no excuses for that Car getting through. If they sight him they're to open fire. Is that understood?"

"Loud and clear."

"Then go to it."

Wade hit his siren, weaving in and out through traffic, Donna's voice relaying his commands. " . . . cars thirty through thirty-five, close off the entire area around the cemetery. All roadblocks on special alert. Hold your positions. Open fire upon confirmed sighting . . ."

Lauren edged farther down the dirt path, The Car's revving engine rising and falling in a raging, earsplitting rhythm. She focused hard on the amber wind-shield, trying to catch a glimpse of the driver, but the cloudy depths of the glass hid any image from her view.

Abruptly the engine noise died to a rumbling idle, and the sudden change brought Lauren to a stop on the path. She primed herself to dive for cover, her mind sorting the possibilities of what he might be up to. Then she knew—the faint sounds of approaching sirens filled the background and The Car slipped into gear, backed up, and shot away from the cemetery, heading east toward the desert mesas.

As the rising crescendo of sirens filled the air she felt the nervous exhaustion pour into her body. Cheers of joy and blasts from band instruments went up from the children. But as the happy sounds blared about her, all she could see was the still-vivid picture of The Car facing her down at the cemetery gate.

The next moment, Wade pulled up and leapt from his car. Before he was halfway down the path to Lauren, other patrol cars were converging on the scene. Limp from the ordeal, she leaned into his open arms.

"Thank God," she whispered.

"Daddy! Daddy!" Debbie and Lynn Marie came rushing out from behind the tree and Wade knelt down to receive them, pressing his daughters hard to his chest.

"Is everybody okay?" he asked anxiously.

"We're fine!" Lynn Marie said excitedly. "Lauren and Aunt Margie saved us!"

"You should have seen her!" Debbie said, turning to look up in wide-eyed admiration at Lauren. "She stood out here and really gave that car what-for."

"She cussed him out *so bad!*" Lynn added. "She really let him have it."

Wade stood up, his expression communicating all that had to be said to Lauren. By now, the cemetery was alive with running, excited children, the mothers and teachers too caught up in the aftermath of the events to make any attempt at organization.

"Take the kids to my house and stay there till you hear from me," he said to Lauren.

She nodded. "He went east, toward the desert."

"Good; he'll run right into one of our roadblocks. I'm on my way back to the station."

"Are you going to get him, Daddy?" Debbie asked.

He reached down and ruffled the little girl's hair. "Yeah, honey, I'm going to get him."

Before Lauren could say anything, he hurried back to his car. He was firing instructions into the mike as he pulled away.

The Car traveled fast across the arid plain, a black smudge on a mute, barren landscape. It moved determinedly, in an attitude not so much of flight as of single-minded progress toward some definite goal.

At his roadblock position, Ray Mott leaned against the side of his car, shotgun in hand, his eyes describing an ever-widening arc across the flat expanse of scrub brush and sand that stretched before him. He was tense with the possibility of a confrontation, toying with the idea of how he'd react, when a pinpoint on the horizon suddenly became alive.

He wiped his right hand on his trousers, removing the thin veneer of sweat from his trigger finger, and squinted into the distance.

There it was again, the same movement, only more

pronounced this time. He judged the object to be at least three miles away but moving at a good clip, the haze around it slowly defining itself into a gathering cloud of dust.

Ray opened the door of his patrol car and slid behind the wheel, snatching the mike from the dashboard.

"Donna, this is Ray. You there?"

"Yeah, Ray. Got something?"

Wade ran into the station just as Ray's voice filtered across Donna's radio.

"Something's coming up fast through Carter's Field. Might be our man, might not. But there's no road there, so whoever it is, he's coming through the scrub. I can't really see him yet; could just as easily be a truck."

"This is Wade, Ray. I'm at the station. Stay in contact until you've got verification."

"Roger. It's coming right this way. Gotta be a four-wheeler."

Ray held the shotgun firmly with his left hand, the stock propped against his thigh. Then he felt his stomach muscles tighten as he caught slices of color from the approaching vehicle.

"It's black."

"Car or truck?" Wade asked urgently.

Ray's mouth went dry with fear. "Oh, Jesus."

"What it it, Ray? What's happening?"

"It ain't no truck. It's him. It's gotta be him."

A little tremor swept through Donna as she and Wade waited for Ray's next words.

"He's on the road now," Ray said. "He'll be here in just a few seconds. Christ! Here we go!"

"Take him out, Ray!" Wade yelled into the mike. "Get him! Blow him away!" Wade heard himself shouting the orders to kill. He heard the intensity of his command and waited for the questioning guilt to come, but it never did.

Ray dropped his mike on the seat, slid out, and raised his shotgun. The index finger of his right hand curled firmly around the trigger.

The Car bore down on him, holding to its collision course.

A rivulet of sweat trickled down Ray's side beneath his shirt. He'd never killed anyone before. In fact, he'd never had to fire a gun in the line of duty. But he was an excellent marksman, and he tried furiously to divorce his mind from the nature of his target.

Unexpectedly, The Car dropped its speed quickly and came to a stop about a hundred feet away, idling calmly.

Ray held his ground, then became aware of Wade's voice crackling over the radio. He had a moment of hesitation, wondering whether to pick up the mike and communicate, but he knew the awkward maneuver would only put him at a disadvantage. Besides, Wade had said to take him out, and that's just what Ray was prepared to do.

The Car sat and waited, the hypnotic idle of its engine a dare for the deputy to do something.

Ray took steady aim at the murky windshield, telling himself over and over that he was only following orders. Then, from some deep corner of his mind, an automatic reflex took charge and he pulled the trigger.

The sound of the gunfire echoed in his ears; the recoil of the powerful gun traveled through the stock and into his firmly braced shoulder. The deputy was ready to jump aside if the impact of the shell sent the dead man's foot stomping spastically on the accelerator.

At first, Ray thought he was functioning in slow motion as he stood there waiting for the glass to blow out, to shatter into a thousand different shards and expose the bloodied, mangled face of the driver.

But nothing happened.

The Car remained just as it had, sitting calmly, not the slightest mark on it anywhere to indicate that it had even been touched.

Could he have missed? The thought was almost meaningless to Ray, but he couldn't deny the evidence that sat in front of him. He banished the idea from his mind, the barrel of his weapon sighted directly on the driver's side of the windshield. This time, he told himself, there would be no doubt, and he fired again.

Wade and Donna stared at the speaker, the sound of their breathing marking the seconds until they would hear Ray's voice.

Numbly, Ray slid behind the wheel of his patrol car and picked up the mike from the seat. The Car glared at him, its black hulking body still unmarked. In a trance of disbelief, the deputy pressed the button and spoke.

"I missed him." Even as he said it, he knew the words were only a feeble attempt at the truth.

Wade couldn't accept what he was hearing. "You're a crack shot. How the hell could you miss a target like that?"

Ray's anger snapped him back to reality. "Shit! I fired twice at point-blank range and nothing happened! He's just sitting there, waiting for me to try it again. And, goddamnit, I'm gonna make him happy!"

But before Ray could move, The Car suddenly

revved its engine once, shifted into reverse, U-turned, and screamed off in the opposite direction.

"He's leaving! The bastard's turned around, heading north on Casper Road!"

"Follow him! We'll box him in! Just stay with him and tell us where he's going! All units, stand by!"

Ray slammed his door shut, shot across a patch of scrub to Casper Road, and sped off after the fast-receding shape of The Car.

XIX

The two cars raced across the plain, Ray's speedometer hugging the one-hundred mark. He knew he could go only another fifteen or twenty miles per hour at most before he'd be running the risk of throwing a bearing and blowing his engine all to hell.

"One-five to station, one-five to station. Do you copy?"

"Go ahead, Ray," Wade said.

"We're still on Casper, but I'm losin' this mother real quick. You got anybody in the area?"

Wade turned to the relief map, taking quick note of the assigned positions of the other roadblocks.

"Thirty-two, intercept on Casper Road. Go!"

Metcalf and Berry, in car thirty-two, jammed onto the highway, leaving a truck driver slowing for their roadblock staring after them in bewilderment.

"This is car thirty-two. We should intersect with Casper Road in about two minutes."

"Twenty-seven, assist the pursuit. Go!"

Denson and MacGruder swung car twenty-seven into a tight U-turn near a shopping center and headed for the outskirts of town, radioing confirmation back to the station.

"Listen, twenty-seven," Wade said, his eyes fixed on the map. "Head out toward Mesa Road and tie in with Metcalf and Berry! Move! Everybody move!"

Wade handed the mike to Donna. "I'm not doing anybody any good sitting here. Just keep your eyes on that map and keep everybody hustling. It's all yours."

Force of habit sent him running out to the rear parking lot, where he stopped short, realizing that his car was out in front. Not wanting to waste any time, he commandeered the nearest vehicle—a department motorcycle—and sped off.

Just after Wade left, Luke straggled in from a side entrance, heard the updates from the pursuit cars coming across the radio, and slumped quietly at a desk, burying his head in his arms.

Denson and MacGruder wove their car through the streets, the town with its densely packed buildings quickly giving way to the sparse structures of the suburbs.

Neither man spoke; their thoughts were leaping ahead to the coming confrontation.

Ray's car was topping out at one-fifteen, the engine whining in protest. All his instincts told him to let up, but he couldn't obey. He knew that if he could just hang in for thirty or forty more seconds, Metcalf and Berry would be in a position to intercept. The steering wheel vibrated in his grip and he found himself gently cajoling his machine to keep up the pace.

"Attention all pursuit cars." Donna's voice carried the firm edge of command. "Wade's on his way out. You still holding on, Ray?"

The Car slipped out of view around a bend in the road.

"Shit! I just lost sight of him! He must be near the Mesa Road intersection by now. Christ knows where he's gonna go from there, but he sure as hell ain't gonna wait around for us."

But, at the foot of the mesa from which Mesa Road took its name, The Car *was* waiting patiently, as if it had nothing to fear from the men giving chase.

Ray's car screamed down the road. "This is one-five. I'm approaching the intersection." He let up on the accelerator, foot poised over the brake pedal, ready to go into a lock-skid if he had to take the intersecting road.

"I see him!" He slammed on the brakes, the screech of the tires almost drowning out his excited voice. "Jesus, I see him! He's at the foot of the mesa. And he's stopped! The sonofabitch is playing games with us!"

"Charge him! Charge him!" Wade yelled into his mike over the roar of the Harley's engine, the wind whipping past his body.

The Car suddenly jumped into action, speeding up the narrow, two-lane highway that wound to the top of the mesa.

Metcalf, Berry, Denson, and MacGruder pushed their vehicles to the limit, bearing down on the Mesa Road intersection, adrenaline pumping with the thrill of the chase.

The Car continued to climb up the mesa. Ray's voice boomed excitedly over the radio. "We got him! He's gonna trap himself! It's just a matter of time, and that bastard's gonna be all ours."

Ray knew the topography well, and as he neared the top of the mesa he couldn't resist gloating at his impending victory.

"That sucker's had, for sure. Ain't no way down but *straight* down. The rest of you guys better stand on it if you wanna join the fun."

Brimming with confidence, Ray skillfully maneuvered around a tight curve. Coming up on the fourth and final turn, he glanced quickly at the shotgun at his side. This time he was going to nail that lunatic, and that's all there was to it.

He slid into the curve and, as he came out on the straightaway that led directly to the top of the mesa, he hit the brakes and veered to his right toward the narrow shoulder at the edge of the precipice—the only way to save himself from crashing head-on into the black Car, which had turned to face Ray and had positioned itself directly in his path.

Fighting for control, he came to a broadsided stop dangerously close to the fifteen-hundred-foot drop. An instant later, The Car sprang forward, pinning Ray's door shut.

"Ray! Ray! What's happening?" Donna's nervous plea went unanswered as he stared down the long hood of The Car. Functioning purely on instinct, he dove for the passenger door. He ripped once at the handle, but nothing happened. He made a desperate grab at the depressed lock button, but as it clicked up he felt a surge of steady movement as The Car bulldozed his vehicle to the brink of the mesa, like a child playing with a toy.

Ray flung open the passenger door and his head reeled as he gaped into the sheer drop that waited for him.

Scrambling back to the driver's side, he felt the hard lines of the shotgun against his leg. The radio was a jumbled mass of agitated voices as he swung the gun around, propping the barrel on the ledge of his open window. He squeezed off two quick rounds and The Car revved its engine in a mocking reply, untouched by the volley. Then it nudged Ray's right rear wheel over the edge. The patrol car listed sharply.

"Jesus! Don't! Please!" He pulled back the rifle and lunged for the open window.

Like an ungainly diver, Ray's car slid out into space, tumbling end over end, slamming the deputy's body against dashboard, roof, and door panels. After an eternity of seconds the free-falling assemblage of metal and glass hit the ground. It exploded on contact, blasting a crater six feet deep in the soft earth.

XX

As thick black smoke drifted lazily up from the base of the mesa, The Car backed away from the vantage point of its latest kill and sped downhill, its massive form devouring the narrow road as it raced to its next encounter.

The two-man teams of Denson and MacGruder and Metcalf and Berry pressed their cars up the initial incline of the mesa, the sight of Ray's burning car prodding them on and hardening their resolve. They hadn't gone far before they caught sight of their objective flashing around a curve above them.

"Mother of Christ," Denson said, "there he is."

MacGruder picked up the mike. "Metcalf, close it up. We can't give that bastard any running room at all."

Metcalf pulled his patrol car up alongside Mac-Gruder's. "You been thinking about this plan of yours for a long time, Mac?" he asked dryly.

"Yeah, about five or six seconds now."

Below the mesa, Wade did some broken-field running on his motorcycle, saving himself a little time but still intersecting with the road a considerable distance behind the two patrol cars.

He pressed the mike close to his mouth, biting off

his words so they could be understood above the din.

"This is Wade! I'm a good two minutes behind you guys, and when I get there I want to find that Car stopped cold! Do you copy?"

The affirmative replies came back quickly and the two teams of men prepared to carry out their assignment.

"Suppose the bastard doesn't stop?" Berry tried to make the remark sound cavalier, but it came out unpleasantly serious.

Metcalf gave him a quick glance from behind the wheel, wondering if the fear showed on his own face as much as it did on his partner's. "He's gotta stop," he said finally.

"Sure. He's gotta."

Racing along side by side, the two patrol cars hit a straightaway about halfway up the mesa, and they hadn't traveled more than twenty yards when The Car surged into view in front of them.

"Hang in there!" MacGruder yelled into his mike. "He'll turn off and then we got him!"

"He keeps saying that like he's done this before," Berry said nervously. "I sure as hell hope he knows what he's talking about."

"Any second now," Metcalf answered. "Just watch."

And as they watched—the gap between the oncoming cars growing smaller with each uneasy breath—what they saw was the beginning of the final few moments of their lives.

The scene unreeled before them with perfect clarity; they comprehended the most minute details of what was happening; and yet, as is often the case with imminent, unavoidable death, they refused to accept it.

With a quickness that denied its imposing size, The Car veered effortlessly to the inside of the road, and for a fraction of a second the four deputies thought it was going to make a vain attempt to swerve around them. But then it was turning again, swinging its bulk across the width of the road in a wrenching lock-skid, throwing itself exactly broadside to the charging patrol cars. Then, as if it had been pried up by an invisible crowbar, The Car left the earth and went into a barrel roll. Once, twice, three times, its down-hill trajectory speeding it downward ever faster with each crunching revolution, The Car became a demonic steamroller heading directly for the twin targets that were the patrol cars.

Desperately hoping to avoid the avalanche of black steel, Metcalf and Denson hit the brakes and tried to swerve their cars out of its path. Denson's car fell slightly behind the other.

In a final act of self-preservation, Berry threw his arms across his face and shut his eyes tightly, his thoughts managing only the first few words of a long-forgotten childhood prayer before his head was filled with the grinding, crumpling sounds of the initial impact.

The Car rolled across the hood of its victim, climbed up and over the windshield and top, and continued across the trunk deck, leaving only a squashed facsimile of the vehicle in its wake, the viscera of the decapitated occupants mingling with the twisted wreck-age.

Coming off its first victim, The Car struck a vicious blow with its revolving snout to the driver's side of Denson and MacGruder's car, sheering off the door and Denson's left leg in the process, and sending the patrol car careening out of control. It spilled over the edge of the mesa and burst into an orange ball of flame.

With one more revolution The Car righted itself. Its horn blasted in excited bursts of victory and then blared in one long, continuous note as it rounded a curve and continued down the road—with not the slightest mark on its glossy black body.

The torch of Denson and MacGruder's car burned brightly in the clear, still air. Wade watched the black monster reach the base of the mesa and straddle the center line of the highway as it roared toward him out of the distance.

Doing sixty on the big Harley, the air whipping past his windscreen and buffeting his legs, Wade felt his rage rise within him to the point where he actually considered sending himself crashing headlong into the charging leviathan in one final act of furious defiance. It was only a tenuous grip on reason that kept him from doing just that, and when a plan that had at least a marginal chance of succeeding finally presented itself to him, he had precious little time to set it into motion.

He let up on the throttle and braked his bike nearly to a stop, giving himself an extra second or two by leaping from the seat at the last moment and letting the Harley skid harmlessly to a halt on the ground off the highway.

Drawing his service revolver, Wade positioned himself in the middle of the road, planted his legs firmly, and took a steady, two-handed aim at the thundering Car.

The closer it came the more viciously the throb of its

engine battered Wade's senses. Every instinct he had told him to run, reminded him that he was only one man against thousands of pounds of hurtling steel. But he forced himself to hold his ground, determined to get off at least one true shot before he dove out of the way.

But where should he aim? Ray had fired point-blank at the monster and failed. Wade couldn't afford to make that mistake. He raced over his options and then, making his decision, sighted down the barrel of his gun at the left front tire. The Car was bearing down on him with unwavering speed. Wade swallowed once, primed himself for a leap to his right, and began the countdown to the moment when he would squeeze off the shot.

Sunlight danced on the vertical grill of The Car. Thoughts of what it would be like if he didn't move fast enough pricked at Wade's mind, a brutal warning of a brutal death. And the last thing he remembered before the unexpected sound pounced upon his consciousness was a portraitlike image of Lauren and his daughters. Then the squeal of skidding tires penetrated his mind and the stench of smouldering rubber nearly gagged him.

The Car was stopping. Fighting to keep its locomotivelike bulk under control, it slid to a shrieking, nerve-jangling halt.

Wade could barely feel himself breathing as he faced his adversary, a distance of only twenty feet separating them, the stifling silence underlined by the disdainful purr of The Car's idling engine.

Gun still aimed, he didn't make the slightest move. He wanted that thing immobilized, and if it was willing to play sitting target for him, so much the better.

Denying himself any more time to debate his actions, he fired a round into the left front tire.

The jagged tread sucked in the bullet as if it were nothing more deadly than a pebble. Wade fired again, and once more a bullet imbedded itself deep within the rubber. But still nothing happened.

Steadily, he raised his gun to the level of the windshield, aligning it with a point on the driver's side that would send the next shot ripping into bone and brain. He was about to kill a man—not in the heat of a violent struggle, but with the same calculated determination with which he'd swat a fly or crush an invading insect. Yet strangely, it didn't bother him. He wasn't sure if that was something he should be proud of, whether it was courage or the wellspring of an instinct he'd never known he possessed. But either way, he was going to do it.

Perhaps because it was directed at a human being, the explosion that drove the bullet from the gun sounded a hundred times louder than the explosions of the patrol cars had. Before the noise had died from his ears, Wade saw a viscous, oily blotch appear on the windshield, signaling that he'd accomplished his task with admirable efficiency.

Cautiously he took a step toward The Car, and in that fragment of elapsed time he witnessed something that his intellect refused to accept. The stain on the amber windshield shriveled and vanished, leaving a smooth, clean surface in its place.

Stopped cold by what he'd seen, Wade felt a new sensation assail him. It was something he hadn't felt since he was a small child alone in the darkness of his room. Something he thought he'd buried years ago. The fear of the unexplainable.

There was nothing left to do but keep moving

toward The Car. The murmur of its engine called him
forward like a whore in the night.

Approaching the driver's side, he was ready to make
a grab for the door handle as soon as he was within
striking distance. While he walked, he kept his gun
trained on the side window, though for what practical
purpose he no longer knew.

He continued his move toward The Car—and then
stopped in mid-motion with the sudden realization
that its slablike side was devoid of any handle. There
was absolutely no visible means of opening the door.
And while Wade still hesitated, baffled, there was a
soft buzzing sound and the window rolled down some
two inches, exposing a horizontal slash of shadowy
interior.

Acutely aware of the motions of his body, Wade
took another step forward.

Click. The sharp, metallic sound startled him, and
the door edged open ever so slightly.

Keep moving, he told himself. *Get a hand on that
door; rip it open and see how many rounds you can
squeeze off before you're lying dead on the road.*

He was only inches away now, tensed for his final
lunge. Suddenly something flashed at him through the
narrow slit, and the terror slid through him like the
thrust of a sharp blade.

Eyes! Deadly, malevolent eyes that glowed with
a burning incandescence.

And then the door swung open with staggering
force; it was a black wall of steel that slammed into
Wade's chest, stomach, and legs and sent him sprawling to the pavement. His head struck the asphalt
with a solid thud; his gun slid easily from his limp
hand.

Barely conscious, his mind a whirlpool of distorted

images, he thought he heard a laugh—a contemptuous, leaden cackle that made him want to scream. Not out of fear, but out of denial.

Because it had come from The Car.

XXI

The chapel was small and lit only by candles, the quivering illumination of their flames casting a rippling light on the gaunt saints who looked down on the proceedings from stained-glass windows. The exposed beams of the vaulted ceiling disappeared into the blackness above Wade, who sat alone in the first pew, acutely alert to his discomfort in the rigid, wooden seat.

He was vaguely aware of the presence of other people around him, but he had neither the desire nor the energy to turn and see who they were. His head ached horribly, and the nausea had been lodged in his stomach for so long that he was becoming almost used to it. The mournful tones of an organ slid through the air, but it meant nothing to him. It was only another irritant, another intrusion on his grief.

The trappings of death were ludicrous to him, a futile attempt to explain a mindless travesty.

When are they going to begin? He asked himself the question for what seemed like the hundredth time. He just wanted it to be over, to be able to call an end to everything that had led him to this agonizing rite of passage.

Then, from the blackness behind him, he heard the sound of approaching footsteps, and he knew his question had been answered.

The dry wood of the pews creaked as the scattered mourners stood. Wade forced himself to his feet, the simple motion generating new explosions of pain in his head, his eyes clouding over with tears as the six shadowy pallbearers wheeled the flower-laden casket to a halt at the head of the aisle.

A robed figure stepped out to the altar; the pungent aroma of incense filled the air. The ceremony began, but the words were drowned out by the metallic laughter of The Car. Didn't anyone hear it? How could they carry on in its midst?

It grew louder and louder, bouncing off the chapel walls like wild bullets, prying out the fears of a lifetime, telling him the truth—a truth he wanted to reject as a monstrous, unspeakable impossibility.

Enough! He would have none of it! He lurched out into the aisle, lunging for the casket. Immediately he felt the tug of restraining hands from behind. His fists thudded into flesh as he fought his way free, sweeping the floral spray from the top of the casket, prying at the lid to force it open, staring in trembling rage at the waxen face.

"Lauren!"

He screamed her name once, and then awoke to find himself in a Trauma Unit cubicle at Memorial Hospital.

Dr. Pullbrook stood beside his bed, tie loosened, collar opened, a tired smile on his face. "Welcome back," he said.

"Jesus. What happened?" He raised his arm to wipe the cold sweat from his face and saw that his clothing had been replaced by a white hospital gown.

"That's what *we'd* like to know," Pullbrook said. "They found you lying across Mesa Road, unconscious and with a dangerously large lump at the base of your skull."

Wade took a deep breath and winced at the pain in his chest.

"Also a few cracked ribs," Pullbrook added. "All in all, you're an extremely lucky man."

"I can name five others who weren't."

"I know; we found them."

"All of them? Dead?"

Pullbrook gave a grim nod.

"And I'm the one that sent them out."

"What else could you do?"

"I'm sure I'll think of a lot of answers to that over the next few years."

"And none of them will be satisfactory. You were lucky to escape with your life. Leave it at that."

"It was more than luck; it was planned. There's no reason I shouldn't have been wasted out there like the rest of the men."

Hesitantly, Wade told of his encounter with The Car, purposely omitting the details of the three gunshots.

"Then you were close enough to get a look at the driver?"

"No," he answered quickly. "He took me out with his door before I knew what was happening. That's when I hit my head on the pavement."

The flash of the eyes and the leaden cackle were vivid in Wade's memory but he refused to mention them, denying the possibility of what they implied.

Dr. Pullbrook was silent for several seconds, his precise, logical mind searching for a rational explanation.

"And he just left you there," he finally said.

"Right. Now tell me why."

"Perhaps he thought you were dead." The reply satisfied neither of them.

"He didn't take any chances with the others. Why should he with me?"

"In the past two days nine people have died. Nine utterly senseless killings. I don't have an answer for that, and I don't have an answer for why you're alive. The only thing I know is that the person in that car has to be stopped."

Again the image of the glowing eyes skimmed through Wade's mind.

"Well, I'm not going to get much done from a hospital bed. How about getting me my clothes and signing me out?"

"I'll be happy to."

"Good."

"Tomorrow morning."

"Come on, Doc. What the hell can I do here?"

"Get some rest and give us the chance to keep you under observation."

"For what? The bump on my head isn't going to go down overnight."

"Your ribs are taped and you suffered a severe concussion. The X-rays say you're all right, but I want to make sure."

Wade tried to raise himself up and the shooting pain in his head immediately made him drop back onto the pillow.

"Wouldn't have gotten very far, would you?"

"Okay. You made your point."

"I'll send something in for the pain. Right now, you've got some very anxious visitors waiting. But I want you to promise to go easy."

"What else can I do?"

"All right then, I'll see you in the morning."

The doctor pulled back the green curtain that surrounded the cubicle and left. In the hall, Wade could hear the voices of Lauren and some of the deputies. When they came in, Luke kept conspicuously to the back, behind Fats and Chas.

Lauren touched his cheek and kissed him, trying hard to keep from crying with relief.

"You had us pretty worried," she said. "How you doing?"

"A little banged up. Fortunately, I landed on my head."

She fumbled in her purse for a hankie and dabbed at her eyes. "Margie sends her love. She's home with the kids."

"They okay?"

"Pretty good. We played it down as much as we could."

He reached out and squeezed her hand. "How about you?"

"Just awfully thankful, that's all."

He looked at her tear-streaked face and realized how much he needed her. "Me too."

"Well," Fats said awkwardly, "the guys and I just wanted to make sure you were okay. We'll pass the word."

"Hey," Wade said, "thanks for coming."

"No sweat," Chas said.

"The roadblocks back up?" Wade asked.

"Ready and waiting. Everybody's doing double duty and we had to get a few boys from the fire department to replace—"

Wade nodded, freeing Chas from his embarrassing position. "Their families been notified?"

"Yeah," Fats said, "Chas took care of it."

"I'm sorry that came down on you; I should've been around to do it."

"It's done," Chas said quietly. "Forget it."

Just then a nurse entered with an extension phone that she plugged in next to Wade's bed. "This is highly irregular, Sheriff, but Dr. Pullbrook authorized it. Your children are on the line."

She set the phone on Wade's lap and left.

He picked up the receiver and tried to make his voice sound as normal as possible.

"Hello? . . . Oh, hi, Margie. . . . Yeah, I'm fine, really. Doc Pullbrook just wants to keep me here overnight to play it safe. . . . Okay, put them on. And listen, that was a hell of a thing you two did at the cemetery." He glanced up at Lauren, then chuckled at something Margie said. "Yeah, right. I'll send Lauren home to relieve you in a little bit. Thanks for everything."

His children came on, their shaky voices ruining their attempt to be brave.

"Don't *ever* let anything happen to you, Daddy," Lynn Marie said.

"Nothing's going to happen to me. I'm too ornery, you know that."

"Are you really coming home tomorrow?" Debbie asked.

"Yes, honey; I'll see you both tomorrow, I promise."

"We miss you, Daddy," they chorused.

"I miss you, too. Now you be good girls for Aunt Margie, and Lauren will be there in a little while. Sleep tight. I love you."

He hung up the phone and looked up at Lauren. "I guess I volunteered you without asking; I'm sorry."

"Don't be silly. I'll just need someone to drop me

off. When the station got the word you were being brought here, Chas came by and drove me over."

Wade started to thank the Indian but he cut him off. "Don't say anything embarrassing or I'll leave."

"You've got a deal."

"Look," Chas continued, "I hate to bother you with shop talk, but I had to lock up Amos Clements this afternoon. He had a shotgun and was screaming bloody murder because his son got hurt."

"Hurt?"

"At the track. He fell and got a broken arm."

"Anybody else?"

"Tattleman got his leg busted up pretty good by a runaway horse. He'll be out for six to eight weeks. One of the wranglers got a concussion; the other one's taped up like you, but they'll both be okay. I hear all three of them did a damn good job out there."

"Make sure they realize I know it, will you?"

Chas nodded.

"And keep Amos locked up for at least twenty-four hours. We've got enough trouble without him running around loose."

"I know what you mean; he said he was gonna find that car and shoot it up good."

"I've got a feeling we might have a lot more of that kind of thing on our hands."

"There's already talk of a vigilante committee forming," Fats said.

"That's just great. Any idea who's behind it?"

"Not yet," Chas said, "but we'll keep our ears open."

"You do that."

"We gotta be on our way, Chief," Fats said. "You get some rest now, y' hear?"

"See you in the lobby," Chas said to Lauren, and the three men began to leave.

"Luke?" Wade called. Chas and Fats moved self-consciously out into the hall while Luke stood caught at the perimeter of the cubicle.

"Look," Wade said, suddenly very tired. "This really isn't the time or the place, but when I come back tomorrow I'll need a good reason why that parade rehearsal wasn't canceled."

"The answer I'll have tomorrow isn't going to be any better than the one I have today. What can I say? All this killing . . . that Car . . . we're not going to stop it, you know. It's going to keep right on until it's ready to leave. I don't know why it picked us, but it's here, and there's nothing we can do about it. You've got to understand that, Wade. I know I should have canceled the rehearsal, but even if I had, it really wouldn't have changed anything; it just would have showed up somewhere else. The shopping center, the school. Who knows? I . . ." He shrugged helplessly. "That's all I can tell you. If you want my resignation, you've got it."

By the time he finished speaking his voice was barely audible. Lauren reached out and squeezed Wade's arm, a signal for him to let it be.

"Go back to work," Wade said. "We'll talk about it tomorrow."

Luke started to say something, then just turned and left.

When they were alone, Lauren got up and drew the curtain, closing off the cubicle, and then sat back down next to Wade's bed.

"Is Luke's trouble what I think it is?" he asked.

Lauren nodded. "Margie says it started last night, after Ev was killed. She's worried, very worried."

"Christ, nine people are dead and my best friend's killing himself. Everything's falling apart, Lauren, and somehow I wound up with the job of putting it back together again. Except I don't know where to begin. I don't know what to do."

"Get out of it. You've had your warning. Let someone else wrestle with it."

"Ray didn't miss," Wade said absently.

"What?"

He hesitated; then the need to confide in someone he could trust took hold of him.

"I fired two shots into his tire and one into the windshield. Nothing happened. Absolutely *nothing*." He couldn't bring himself to mention the disappearance of the viscous mark on the glass, wondering if perhaps it was something he'd hallucinated after the concussion.

He could see the fear on Lauren's face and he was immediately sorry he'd told her anything.

"The damn thing must be built like a tank," he said, trying to talk away the tension. "But even a tank can be stopped."

"He was toying with us at the cemetery," she said vacantly. "He could have killed us any time he wanted. Why didn't he?"

"Look, this guy's impossible to figure out, so don't waste your time."

"But there's got to be a *reason!* He could have easily crashed through those tombstones and killed us all. In fact, he could have killed us while he was chasing us. It doesn't make any sense. And then there was the wind."

"Wind? What wind?"

"Just before he hit the track the wind came up. Hard. Out of nowhere. And it had a funny sound to it. Sort of, I don't know—just strange, like it really didn't belong."

A thought nagged at the back of Wade's mind, but he couldn't bring it into focus.

"Hey," he said, "you're letting your imagination run wild. Besides, we've got better things to talk about."

"Good. I could use a change of subject. What's on your mind?"

"Us."

"I see. Have you come to any conclusions?"

"Three."

"Three?"

"I love you; I need you; and I want you to marry me."

"I guess a girl can't very well argue with that, can she?"

She bent over him and they kissed, Wade ignoring the pain in his ribs when he put his arms around her.

"I'm sorry I took so long," he said.

She laid a finger on his lips. "I don't care about all that. The important thing is that it's here and we're together."

He kissed her again, and when they parted, concern flickered across her face.

"What's wrong?" he asked. "Having second thoughts already?"

"Please, this is important."

"Okay, what is it?"

"First of all, I want you to understand that I'm *asking* you this. Not telling, just asking."

"Go ahead."

"Wade, forget about chasing that car. Forget about being sheriff. You're alive. That's the way I want to keep you, and that's the way your children want to keep you."

An awkward silence hung between them.

"I can't," he said softly. "If I left now, it'd be with me for the rest of my life. I'm not saying you're wrong. I'm just saying I have to let things take their course. Please try to understand that, because you know I'd never do anything to intentionally hurt you or the girls."

"I know, darling. And as far as I'm concerned, it's settled. But you can't blame me for trying."

"I'd have been worried if you hadn't."

The sound of the curtains being sharply drawn back surprised them, and a stern-looking nurse stood facing them, a hypodermic syringe in her right hand.

"I'm afraid your visitor will have to leave now."

Lauren gave him a quick kiss. "Well, if I'm going to spend the night with the kids, I think I'll have Chas drop me off at my place to get some clothes and things."

"Good idea, and thanks—for everything."

"Thank *you,* and get a good night's rest. We've got a lot of plans to make."

He smiled as she walked past the nurse and out through the door.

"Right arm, please," the nurse said brusquely.

"Hmm?"

"For your injection."

"Oh, sure." He felt the cold alcohol swab and the prick of the needle.

"There," the nurse said. "We'll be in to check you periodically."

She left the curtains open, and as Wade lay there, waiting for the pain to seep from his body, he let his mind drift over the conversation he'd had with Lauren. Then suddenly something snapped into place.

The wind! Lauren had mentioned the wind coming up just before The Car had attacked the parade rehearsal. It had disturbed him at the time, but he hadn't known why.

Now he remembered. The old Navajo woman in the station, right after Ev had been killed and Wade had chased the vanishing taillights into the desert.

He groped in his thoughts for what she'd said about The Car; then her words came back to him.

Bad things, she had said, were coming on the wind.

XXII

Chas was waiting in the lobby near the main entrance when Lauren came down the hall.

"All set?" he asked.

"Yes." She smiled happily. "I am."

"The doctor left this for you," he said, handing her a piece of paper with an illegible scrawl on it. "It's a prescription for some pain pills for Wade. He thought it might be a good idea if you got it filled for him in the morning. Didn't trust the chief to do it himself."

"Sounds like he knows our boy pretty well."

"I don't think I've ever seen him take so much as an aspirin in all the years I've worked with him," Chas said.

"He must think he's part Indian," she teased, and they stepped out into the cool night air, Lauren stuffing the prescription into her coat pocket.

As they drove through the dimly lit streets on the outskirts of town, Lauren said reflectively, "Chas, what do you think of all this?"

"What can I say? It's terrible."

"I mean beyond that, the reason behind it."

"I suppose when you're as crazy as that, you don't need a reason for anything, even murder."

"Then that's all you think it is, a crazy man in a car?"

His hesitation told her she'd hit a nerve.

"Chas, is there something you're hiding from me? Something I'm not supposed to know?"

"You probably know just as much about this thing as I do."

"Then what is it? What's bothering you?"

"Miss Humphries . . ."

"Call me Lauren."

"Okay, Lauren. Maybe this sounds silly to you, but I come from a background that explains nearly everything—life, death, the rising and setting of the sun—by one kind of superstition or another. And as much as I like to tell myself that it's all a bunch of foolish tales, those same tales completely ruled the lives of my ancestors up until just two generations ago. My grandparents all lived well into their nineties, and I can still remember them issuing stern warnings when one omen or another would cross their paths. My parents were caught in the middle, and it was tough for them. But me—I'm supposed to be free from all that."

"And are you?"

"I thought I was, until that Car showed up. Now I don't know."

"Then you have a theory?"

"What good are theories unless they can be proved? I could tell you that that Car was evil, that it was a demon, or driven by one, but would that really change anything? A lot of good people would still be dead, and maybe a lot more would follow. So either way— crazy man or devil—we've got our hands full. The important thing is to stop it."

"But how, Chas? How do you stop something if you don't even know what it is?"

The big Indian shrugged. "I don't know. Maybe you don't; maybe it just goes away when it's had enough."

"That's something we can't afford to wait around and find out."

"That's also something we might not have any choice about."

Chas slowed and glanced at a small trailer parked off the road, two lights burning in the front windows.

"Something wrong?" Lauren asked.

"Just checking on my homestead, that's all." He picked up speed and they moved on through the moon-lit night. "They've been pretty upset lately."

"I didn't know you were married."

"Oh, sure. Even got two kids."

"I think that's wonderful."

He smiled proudly. "So do I."

Turning a corner, he pulled up in front of Lauren's house. It was a modest affair on a dark country road, surrounded by trees and fairly well isolated from surrounding structures.

"Thanks for the ride," she said. "I'm sure you've got better things to do."

"No problem. How long do you think you'll be?"

She stepped out of the car and turned back to face him. "Not long. Come on in and make yourself comfortable."

"No, that's okay."

She could read the concern on his face. "Listen, why don't you go and check on your family, then come back for me in ten or fifteen minutes?"

"You're sure you don't mind?"

"Of course not. Now please, I insist."

"Thanks. I'll make it as fast as I can."

"See you in a little while," she said, and she shut the car door, stepping back as he drove off.

She watched his car disappear into the blackness, glad she'd let him go home and check in with his family, but nevertheless a little uneasy at being left alone.

She reached into her coat pocket to withdraw her keys and the prescription from Dr. Pullbrook fell to the ground, but as she bent to pick it up a sudden flurry of wind blew it from her outstretched fingers. The paper danced down the street, Lauren hurrying after it and finally catching it when the gust of wind subsided.

She walked slowly back toward her house, trying to calm herself, trying to tell herself it was just an ordinary act of nature, that she couldn't go through life fearing something as commonplace as the wind—when it began again.

Lauren stood still in the middle of the street, listening to the rustle of the breeze as it gained intensity. She looked up at the starless sky overhead, saw the tall trees swaying high above her, and felt the panic rising within her.

It was the same, the same unnatural sound that the wind had had at the racetrack! It whipped about her now, tugging violently at the prescription in her hand as if fighting her for it, and she began to run, the swirling air stinging her cheeks, forcing her eyes to squint for sight. Then, from somewhere overhead, she heard a sharp, intense crack and a heavy branch crashed to the ground, its rough bark scraping the sleeve of her coat as it landed only inches from her.

Stumbling ahead, she crossed her lawn and leaned panting against the front door of her house, fumbling frantically for the key. Then she had it, was jamming it into the doorknob, was twisting it to free the lock. And then the howling wind carried a new threat to her ears: the distant thundering of a car.

She lurched into the house, slamming the door behind her, securing the deadbolt and pausing only momentarily to catch her breath before running to the telephone that sat on an end table next to the sofa.

She grabbed the receiver, then realized she didn't even know the number she wanted to call. Hanging up the phone, she dashed across to a bookcase, yanked out the Santa Ynez phone directory, and riffled through the pages until she found the number she was looking for. Repeating it once to herself, she dropped the book and ran back to the phone.

"Memorial Hospital," the singsong voice at the other end of the line said.

"Wade Parent," Lauren said, trying to control her fear.

"Do you have a room number?"

"Oh, what do you call it? The Trauma Unit."

"I'm sorry," the voice said in a maddeningly calm tone, "but patients in that section are not allowed to receive telephone calls."

"Look, damnit! He's the sheriff and this is important! Put me through to the nurse in charge!"

"One moment, please."

There was a click and then a vacuous silence as Lauren was put on hold.

She stood there, her back to a large picture window with the drapes open, the wind still hissing furiously through the trees, unaware, in her impatience with the operator, of the two tiny globes of light that were hanging suspended in the distance.

"Trauma Unit," a voice finally said.

"This is Lauren Humphries. I have to speak to Sheriff Parent. It's urgent."

"I'm sorry, but—"

"Stop being sorry and let me talk to him! This is official business and Dr. Pullbrook won't be very happy if he finds out you've kept me from getting through."

There was a muffled sound as the nurse cupped her hand over the receiver. Lauren stared at the ceiling in frustration, her anger on the verge of outweighing her fear.

Behind her, the twin lights were looming larger in the clear glass of the window.

"Hello?" The man's voice on the line surprised her, and it took her a moment to realize it was Wade.

"Lauren? Is that you?"

"Yes, darling, it's me."

"What's the matter? Where are you calling from?"

"I'm at my place."

"Are you all right?"

"Just listen to me. Please! It's the wind, the same wind that blew at the racetrack today. It came up right after Chas dropped me off."

"Where the hell is he?"

"I told him to go and check on his family. He should be back in just a few minutes. But Wade, I'm scared. That Car is out there somewhere. I just know it is. I think I even heard the engine!"

"All right, just take it easy. I want you to promise me you'll stay in your house until you hear from me. Do you understand?"

"Yes, I promise."

"Okay, now I'm going to call the station and get

some extra men in the area right away. Meanwhile, you *stay right there!*"

But Lauren was only half listening now, because the room was flooding with bright light, light that bounced off the figurines on the bookcase, baffling her with its intensity.

"Lauren? Lauren, answer me!" Wade's persistent voice was far away, then totally eclipsed by the shattering blast of a car horn.

Headlights glaring, the airborne beast exploded through the picture window just as Lauren turned around. Shards of flying glass lacerated her face and blinded her wide, staring eyes. Then the bumpers and grill of the rampaging hellhound reduced her upper torso to human garbage.

Horn still blaring, it continued its flight, rupturing a gaping hole in the facing wall of the house, nosing its descending bulk back to earth and disappearing into the shelter of the night.

Behind, billows of white plaster dust swirled over the wreckage. Splintered timbers, scattered books, overturned pieces of furniture—it was as if the fist of an angry child had punched its way through a doll house. Only the remains of the figure on the floor were tragically real.

XXIII

"Nurse!" Wade screamed the word and his head vibrated with pain. The supervising nurse rushed over to his cubicle.

"What is it, Mr. Parent? What's wrong?"

"Get me my clothes; I've got to get out of here."

"That's impossible. Dr. Pullbrook left strict orders that you were to remain overnight for observation."

Wade still held the phone receiver in his hand, and he clutched it so tightly his knuckles blanched white with the pressure.

"Look, lady, the next call I make is to the Sheriff's Department to have them send a car for me, and when it gets here I'm leaving, with or without my clothes. So if you want to make it easy on yourself you'll wake up Dr. Pullbrook and tell him what's happening. The choice is yours."

Without waiting for a reply, Wade viciously dialed the phone number of the department. It rang once. Thompson, working the night shift, handled the call.

"Sheriff's Department. Deputy Thompson speaking."

"Hal, this is Wade. We've got a possible sighting of The Car in the vicinity of Elm and Chestnut. I want the area flooded with men immediately. Next, get on the horn to Chas—he's at his house—and tell him to get his ass over to Lauren's right away. You better send an ambulance, too. And I want a car over here to pick me up, Code Three. I'll be waiting in front of the main entrance."

"Jesus, did something happen to Lauren?"

"No questions, Hal, just do it! Now!"

Wade slammed the phone down and glared at the nurse who still stood beside his bed.

"Well, how about it? Do I get my clothes or don't I?"

"I'm sorry," she said softly. "I mean, if anything else has happened."

Wade could only nod, afraid that if he answered his emotions would overtake him.

"I'll get your clothes," the nurse said, and she left him alone.

He stood outside the hospital and waited. He was oblivious to everything except those last few seconds on the phone with Lauren, and he replayed them over and over again: the fear in her voice, his frustration at not being able to be there with her, the agony that had shot through him when he heard the sickening sound of the horn blaring across the phone. Then the terrible crash and the swift, indelible silence that had swallowed up her name as he'd shouted it time after time into the mute receiver.

Why?

He knew that was the question he would ask himself forever, the single word that would lead him through a maze of half-truths, deceptions, rationalizations, and, most certainly, despair. And in the end, he knew he would always come up with a large handful of nothing, a ladle of water from a brackish well that would quench his thirst only temporarily and leave him with the wracking pain of his endless search.

So much had been waiting for them, a ribbon of

experiences they could have shared together, the two of them almost a single person. And in the space of one brief telephone call it had all been snatched away from him—from them—obliterated by . . . by what? There was another question to taunt him. Just what *was* this Car? Where had it come from? Who was driving it and what was the hate that consumed him, forcing him to wreak his terrible, aimless vengeance on Santa Ynez?

He remembered Lauren's words as she'd talked about The Car at his bedside. *He was toying with us,* she'd said. *He could have killed us all any time he wanted to.* Christ, what kind of a game was this that had already taken so many lives—and why wasn't he one of the corpses?

His head pounded with the unanswered questions. Then, in the background, he heard the wail of a siren. It was a lonely sound, floating through the still night, and Wade couldn't help identifying with its plaintive call and wondering if the driver of The Car heard it too.

It grew louder and he let it wash through his mind, driving out for at least a few peaceful seconds the haunting specter of reality. Then he saw the flashing red lights coming down the street, slowing as they approached the hospital, and a few seconds later a sheriff's car pulled up in front of him, the siren grinding to a dying halt.

The man inside reached across and opened the door, and as Wade bent to get in he saw Luke's face in the dim illumination of the dashboard.

He settled in next to his friend and closed the door. "Let's go," he said, "and keep the siren."

Luke gunned the car away from the curb and the siren shrieked to life.

"Chas called in while I was on my way over." Luke's voice was choked with emotion.

Wade said nothing, simply stared straight ahead through the windshield.

"She's gone," Luke said, almost to himself. "Goddamnit! She's gone!" Then he started to cry, giving vent to the kind of grief that isn't a release, only an added dimension of pain. Large, wrenching sobs heaved from his body, tears clouding his vision as he sped through the deserted streets.

Wade turned and looked at him, wondering when his own breaking point would come, almost wishing he didn't have the strength to continue.

Gradually Luke pulled himself together, wiping his eyes with the sleeve of his shirt.

"I'm sorry, Wade. I'm so sorry for you. For everybody. It's been so much. So damn much."

"I know."

"Margie's with the kids. I left word at the station not to tell her anything."

The two men sat in stoic silence; then Wade spoke.

"Do you think you can make it?" he asked.

"I really don't know. I haven't done a very good job so far, have I?"

"You did a perfect job for five years."

"That was different."

"Why?"

"I had things I could rely on. The security of a routine. When I went to sleep at night I knew what to expect the following day. Now it's all been pulled out from under me."

"From *you?*" Wade yelled. "You're still alive! You still have your wife! Or don't they count for anything?"

"Please, don't."

"The hell I won't! You're killing yourself, and I've

seen enough death in the last two days. Christ, you might as well go and lie down in front of that fucking black Car and get it over with! Is that what you want?"

"No!"

"Then why are you doing this?"

"You really don't understand what's happening, do you? How many people have to die before you'll accept the truth?"

The malevolent, burning eyes hovered in Wade's mind, but he willed them away. "The only truth I know is that there's a killer loose and it's my job to stop him."

"If that's all there is to it, then why is that Car still out there? Think about it! Why do people kill, Wade? You've been with the department for over ten years; you know the answer just as well as I do: greed, jealousy, revenge, self-preservation. I could list a dozen reasons for taking someone's life. And as cheap and as shallow as they'd all be, at least they'd be *motives*. But do any of them apply to your so-called killer?"

"I don't know," he answered quietly.

"You know. You just don't want to admit it." Luke sighed. "Not that I blame you. We're both doing the same thing; the only difference is that you don't need any booze to help you along. Jesus Christ Almighty, I wish I could take you and Margie and your kids and get us all as far away from here as possible, but I'm not even sure that would do any good."

"Running away isn't going to stop that Car."

"*Nothing's* going to stop that Car, and the sooner you admit it, the better off we'll all be!"

"All right! Believe what you want! I'm not saying I know all the answers behind this thing. But I *am* saying that I need your help, and I need you *sober*. So make up your mind, Luke, because one thing I haven't got right now is time."

"Give it up, Wade! Take your kids and get the hell out while you still have a chance. Maybe you'll get lucky; maybe you'll buy yourself some time. You told me to be thankful I'm still alive—well, I'm telling you the same thing. So you're the sheriff; who gives a damn? You inherited the job from a dead man. Why are you in such a hurry to join him?"

Wade didn't answer, because looming ahead of them on the road was a cluster of flashing red and blue lights. He hadn't realized that they'd turned onto Lauren's street, but now that they were there, he felt afraid. Afraid of what he was about to witness, and afraid that it would destroy him.

XXIV

Luke pulled the patrol car into the crisscross of official vehicles and switched off the ignition. The revolving light atop the ambulance lent a ghastly illumination to Wade's face as he looked through the passenger window at the wreckage that lay before him.

His first impression was one of awe at the sheer immensity of what The Car had wrought. The tidy wooden fence that surrounded the property ran in a neat, straight line and then suddenly terminated in jagged, raw ends, leaving a gap of some nine or ten feet before resuming its progress around the small plot of land. The lawn stretched unmarked to the broad expanse of what had been the picture window but was now a rectangular void in the front of the house, razor-sharp icicles of glass clinging to the edges of the frame and glinting with the colored lights of the vehicles gathered on the street. And beyond, only partially visible from Wade's angle, was the brutal hole in the back wall, gross and uneven like the wound inflicted by a .45. The hole admitted a gentle, incongruous glow of moonlight.

Mechanically, Wade's head reached for the door handle and pulled it up. He was vaguely aware of the sound of the disengaging lock; as he pushed the car door outward, Chas walked up and stopped it with his hand.

"Don't go in," he said.

Wade looked up at him, his eyes steady and unblinking, and Chas released the door, averting his gaze in shame and grief as Wade walked past him across the lawn and stopped at the obliterated picture window.

The room was desolate, furniture and artifacts scattered about like discards tossed casually into a throwaway box. He spotted her purse among the debris, then stepped up onto the frame of the window and entered the room.

Broken pieces of glass cracked beneath his shoes as he walked toward the bloodstained sheet, his unwavering stare recording the crablike scuttle of the ambulance attendants as they moved out of his path. The anxious babble of voices somewhere behind him receded to a dim, meaningless murmur.

He didn't know how long he stood over her covered form, but then he felt himself sinking to his knees, drawn down like a stick in a whirlpool. He saw that his hand was trembling as he reached out for the sheet, grasping it by the edge, lifting it slowly back to expose . . .

He heard a sound, a low, heartbreaking moan, and then he realized that it had come from him. A drop of cold sweat fell from his forehead, dripping onto the back of his hand. With a reverence he'd never known he possessed, he laid the sheet back in place. Then he forced himself to stand, his legs two shaky foreign objects beneath him, and managed to find a chair that had somehow been left upright in the midst of the rubble.

There was nothing left to do but sit, sit and watch as they carried her away.

Number ten.

Only this time, the body in the litter might just as well have been his.

XXV

"Wade." The voice floated down through his grief from somewhere above and he raised his head to see Chas standing over him. The large, brawny Indian looked somehow frail as he stood in the crumpled surroundings of the living room.

"I should have stayed with her," Chas said. "If I hadn't left her . . ."

"You'd be dead too," Wade interrupted, his words flat and hard. "And I'd have one less man to help me stop that Car."

"But if I'd been here, maybe we could have gotten out."

"It was the wind," Wade said.

"What?"

"She was on the phone to me when it happened. She said the wind had come up. The same thing happened just before they were attacked at the racetrack. She only had a few seconds; there was nothing you could have done."

Luke came in, surveyed the wreckage, and cursed softly. Then he turned to Wade. "Dan Garrett's outside. He knows it's lousy timing, but he has to talk to you."

"I was expecting him," Wade said, and he stood up wearily.

"I can tell him you're just not up to it," Luke offered.

"I'm glad he's here," Wade said. "I need to find out where I stand. And if I'm still sheriff, you two and all the other deputies better think twice about whether you want to stay on the job. Because one way or the other, I'm going to stop that Car. Permanently."

"Listen to me," Luke said urgently. "It can't be done."

"Then stay out of it," Wade said bitterly. "I told you on the way down here you had a choice to make. Do as you damn please, Luke, but don't try to change my mind."

Wade stepped past him and headed for the enormous hole in the back wall.

"I know why he didn't go into the cemetery," Luke said, and Wade stopped and looked back at him.

"It was hallowed ground," Luke said quietly. "There was no other reason for it. There couldn't be."

Wade refused to let himself accept the solution, because accepting it would mean defeat, and that was something he wasn't prepared for, not with Lauren gone.

"I'm not buying it," Wade said, "and I can't believe that you are either." He started to walk away again.

"I'm telling you, Satan is in that Car," Luke said steadily.

Wade stopped but wouldn't turn around, afraid of where the discussion might lead him.

"When I was a boy," Chas said very quietly, speaking more to himself than anyone else, "when my grandfather said the sun would shine the next morning, it shined. When he said it would rain, it rained. Before the dogs howled, he knew if someone was going to die.

I remember. And I asked him once *how* he knew. He looked at me, his leathery old face breaking into a smile, and he said, '*Now* you're asking the right questions.' Then he poked his finger into the air all around him and he said, 'We are not alone here. The others—they know; they hear; they tell me.' "

Chas shifted self-consciously. "Don't ask me what it means. But somehow, the old man was always right."

Wade turned back to them for the final time, his face cold and immovable. "I'm not here to sit and listen to a lot of damn talk. I want the roadblocks up and the rest of the men down at the station. Is that clear?"

"You're a fool," Luke said. "How did The Car know where Lauren lived? Everyone else was killed on the street; she was killed in the safety of her own living room. Doesn't that tell you something? She was special! It wanted her because she cursed it! That's why it didn't kill you out on Mesa Road. It wanted you alive —alive to suffer Lauren's death. It's beyond us, Wade. It's too much for you to fight. Too much for any of us."

"I'll see you at the station," he said, and he walked through the jagged hole into the night.

Dan Garrett was waiting for Wade in front of the house, looking tired and angry, and everyone was careful to keep their distance. When he saw Wade approaching, Garrett walked over to intercept him, isolating them on the front lawn.

"I'm sorry this had to happen," Dan said.

"So am I. Now let's get down to business. Am I still sheriff?"

"I don't want any vendettas, Wade. That's not going to solve anything."

"Do you want that Car stopped or don't you?"

"Of course I do."

"Fine. Now you still haven't answered my question. Am I sheriff?"

"As far as I'm concerned you are."

"Meaning what?"

"Fear travels fast. There's been an emergency session of the town council called, open to the public. It starts in half an hour."

"So the headhunters are out. Is that what you're trying to tell me?"

"They're scared. And when people are scared, they do foolish things."

"I'm not interested in their motives," Wade said. "I just want to know if they're going to win."

"Not if I can help it. But it's going to be one hell of a tough fight, I can tell you that."

"Tell me something else. Why are you on my side?"

"Because I don't think there's a man around who can do a better job. Pure and simple."

Wade took a deep breath of the night air, his tightly taped chest throbbing with pain.

"Get me forty-eight hours, Dan. That's all I'm asking."

"You're worth more than forty-eight hours to this town. A hell of a lot more."

"Maybe. Maybe not. We can talk about that afterward. Right now, I want that Car."

"We all do."

"Then there's one important condition. If they give me the time, they give it to me with no strings, or they can keep it."

"I think that's something it's better to leave unspoken unless they bring it up."

"Do what you have to. You're the politician. Just get me my time."

"I meant what I said about vendettas."

"No strings, Dan. Remember?"

The mayor stared at the ground for a moment, then looked back at Wade. "Okay. No strings."

"Good."

"Don't jump to conclusions. What the council agrees to and what the people do might be two different things. I understand Karl Jenkins is making noises about forming a vigilante committee."

"I know," Wade said.

"He's sure to be at the meeting, and with the mood of this town, they're going to be very receptive to what he has to say."

"I don't want to tell you how to run your show," Wade said, "but maybe it wouldn't be a bad idea to give him a little slack."

"The question is, how much?"

"Let him get some volunteers with CB rigs. They can patrol their own streets and keep in touch with each other. There must be at least one or two of those CB channels that are open to police calls. If they see anything, they can holler."

"Not a bad idea," Dan said.

"They're going to be out there anyway, no matter what we tell them, so they might as well feel they're with us instead of against us."

"Don't kid yourself," Dan said. "Right now, everybody's against us." He glanced at his watch. "I'd better get moving."

"I'm counting on you," Wade said.

"Don't worry. You'll get your time if I have to lock 'em in the goddamn hall. But that Car sure as hell better be gone when they get out, or the headhunters are going to have two of us to chase."

The big man walked away, leaving Wade to grapple

with the idea of his self-imposed time limit, to wonder if he could make good his end of the bargain. He was concentrating so heavily on what lay ahead of him that he almost failed to notice the patrol cars beginning to pull away.

He jogged to the curb and his head reeled with the pain of his strides.

Luke was standing by Chas's car; the Indian was just getting ready to pull away.

"Garrett give you a rough time?" he asked.

"That's not important," Wade said to Luke. "I want you to double up with Chas. I'm taking your car back myself."

"You're in no shape to drive, Wade."

"Goddamnit, don't tell me what shape I'm in. Give me the keys. That's an order."

Luke looked hard at his friend, wishing he'd listen to reason but knowing it was useless. Grudgingly, he handed him the car keys. Wade took them and Luke suddenly grabbed his wrist. The two men glared at each other angrily.

"That wasn't the booze talking inside," Luke said. "I knew exactly what I was saying and I meant every word."

"I heard you the first time. Now let me go."

"For God's sake, Wade, let it be. Think of your children."

Wade swung with his left, his fist catching Luke hard across the jaw and sending him sprawling into the street.

Chas started to get out of his car, but saw there was nothing to do. The two men just glared at each other. Then Luke stood up, walked around to the passenger side of Chas's car, and got in.

Within moments Wade was alone. Slowly, his legs

began to carry him to the empty, violated house. He entered through the front door, turned sharply to his right, and stood on the threshold of the demolished living room.

After his own confrontation with The Car, he had dreamed of Lauren's death. Now it was a reality, and his life was halved. He could do as Luke had pleaded. He could take his children and run, but that would only guarantee a slower death for all of them, and it would leave Lauren a dishonored, forgotten statistic.

He stepped into the room then and his glance fell on her purse, which still lay on the floor. As he looked at it, and thought of how she'd had it with her not an hour before at his bedside in the hospital, that simple object somehow conjured her to the point where he wanted to reach out and touch her.

But there was only emptiness, and he wept.

XXVI

The town council chambers at City Hall were packed to overflowing, the one hundred and fifty seats having long ago been filled. People crammed the two aisles, spilling out into the corridor. Children who had been roused from a sound sleep, many of them still in their pajamas, sat in their parents' laps or were held wearily by those unfortunate enough to have to stand. Dozens of different arguments raged simultaneously, sending up a babble of voices that grated on the nerves and only served to edge an already neurotic crowd closer to the brink of mass hysteria.

As president of the council, Dan Garrett had been closeted with the six other members in an adjoining caucus room for ten minutes, during which time he had been using his considerable powers of persuasion to convince them that Wade should be retained as sheriff for at least the next forty-eight hours.

Since they'd all had the foresight to get up to the caucus room by way of a concealed rear stairway, their presence was as yet unknown to the crowd. But they certainly knew that the crowd was out there, and the frightened, angry voices that boomed through the paneled walls weren't doing anything to help Dan's argument.

"Listen to them," Sam Cunningham said, afraid to speak above a moderate whisper despite the fact there was no chance he could be heard amid the clamor in the council chambers. "If we go out there and try to feed them another forty-eight hours of Wade Parent, it'll take a riot squad to quiet them down."

"It's not just Wade," another councilman said, "it's the whole idea of sticking them with the status quo. They want a change; that's the only thing that's going to pacify them."

"Like who?" Dan challenged. "You want to appoint one of those frightened, pathetic people sheriff?"

"Of course not."

"Okay," Dan prodded, "then let's look in the department. Give me the name of one deputy strong enough to step into a situation like this and not be ground up by it before the week's out."

"And what's the guarantee that Wade won't be?" Sam Cunningham asked.

"He's got a *motive*. He wants that Car, and he wants it bad."

"To keep his job?" one of them asked.

"To keep his sanity, I suspect," Dan answered.

"What are you talking about?"

"The school teacher, Lauren Humphries. I did a little checking. She was at the hospital this evening, and she placed an emergency call to him a little while after she left. I had it traced, and it came from her house. That means she was probably on the phone to him when she died."

"Jesus," Sam said, and for the first time there was silence among the councilmen.

"*Now* can you give me the name of anybody better equipped to fight that Car?"

"It's still going to be an uphill fight to sell it to that crowd," Sam said.

"You're damn right it is," Dan said. "But if we let them yell long enough and loud enough, they'll eventually wear themselves down."

"Unless they wear us down first."

"They won't if we go out there in agreement that they won't," Dan said. "We've had our differences in the past, gentlemen, but this is one time when we've got to stay together. Because if we don't, we're going to turn this town over to anarchy. I don't think any of us wants to live with that for the rest of his life."

No one could deny his point.

"All right then," he said, "let's get this thing started. I have a feeling we've got a long night ahead of us." And with that, he yanked open the door to the caucus room and stepped out into the pandemonium in the council chambers.

Wade sat at his desk at the station, his deputies surrounding him, many of them sipping hot coffee from white styrofoam cups. They all tried very hard to look as if they were simply involved in a routine briefing, but there was little they could do to hide their concern and tension as they digested Wade's plan.

"I don't like it," Chas said. "You're setting yourself up."

"That's the whole point," Wade answered calmly.

"There's no way we can cover you on something like this," Hal Thompson said.

"I'm not asking for cover, Hal."

"Then you're asking to be killed," Luke said, and Wade didn't answer.

"Suppose he doesn't show up?" Chas asked.

"He'll show."

"Why? What makes you so sure?"

"Because he wants me, and I want him. And we both know it."

"So you're going to throw yourself out there like a piece of meat and hope he grabs the bait," Luke said. "I think you're crazy."

Wade looked at the men. "Anybody who wants out can leave right now, no questions asked."

Nobody moved, then Wade turned to Chas. "Go get Amos."

The Indian nodded, glad for an end to the discussion, and headed for the corridor that led to the small jail area.

Amos was asleep on his cot and Chas gave one of the rickety legs a swift kick to bring the prisoner around.

"Hey!" Amos sat up, his eyes bleary with sleep. "What the hell's goin' on?"

"Get up," Chas said. "You're gettin' out."

"Well it's about time! You bastards are gonna regret the day you put me in here. I oughta sue all your asses for false arrest!"

The next thing Amos knew, a powerful hand clamped on his shirt front and lifted him to his feet, making him rise on his tiptoes to come within eye level of the big Indian.

"Shut your mouth and follow me," Chas said. "You think you can do that? Or do you want some help?"

Amos had sense enough to keep quiet and Chas reluctantly released his grip.

Morosely, Amos followed the deputy down the short corridor and into the station room, where the others looked up at him with a kinship that made him at once uneasy.

"Gimme my keys and wallet," he said, but his voice

lacked the bite it usually had, and he was greeted by a wall of silence.

"Sit down," Chas ordered.

Reluctantly, Amos pulled up an empty chair and sat, his eyes darting back and forth across the cluster of men.

"What's this all about?" he asked. "Are you letting me go or aren't you? I didn't commit no crime, you know. You want to lock somebody up, go get that bastard in the black Car before he kills somebody else."

"He already has," Wade said evenly, and Amos stared at the floor, the increasing number of deaths touching even him.

"Who?" he asked, his head still bent.

Wade said nothing, and Amos slowly raised his head.

"Here's what we're going to do," Wade said, and he proceeded to outline his plan.

XXVII

Dan Garrett brought the sturdy gavel down hard on the oak table, pounding it over and over again while he called for order with his booming voice. But the angry crowd continued their shouts and jeers, and the only thing he could do was wait until they calmed themselves down.

It had been going like this ever since Dan and the councilmen had stepped into the chambers. The initial demonstration had lasted almost a full five minutes, and when he'd finally been given a chance to speak and had told them that Wade was to remain sheriff for forty-eight hours, he'd been met with another wave of protest.

The pattern had been repeating itself for more than half an hour now, and Dan knew if he didn't restore some semblance of order soon, the six councilmen who were ranged three on each side of him would lose what little resolve they had and give in to the demands of the frightened, irrational crowd.

Suddenly Dan was on his feet, muscling his way down an aisle and standing face to face with Karl Jenkins, the leader of this latest outburst.

Had his action been directed at anyone other than Karl, Dan would have only incensed the crowd further by coming down among them. But they knew both men for what they were—rugged, tough-minded individualists—and the formidable challenge of the face-off gradually quieted the noisy throng.

"Now," Dan said firmly, "are we going to talk or conduct a circus?"

"You're the one who's made it a circus by trying to ram Wade Parent down our throats. These people want action."

"We're willing to listen, but that doesn't include being threatened or given ultimatums."

Someone in the back shouted an obscenity and Karl wheeled around, anxious for whoever it was to try it again. But there wasn't a sound. Slowly, he turned back to Dan.

"We're ready," Karl said, and Dan walked back to the head of the room, thankful his gamble had worked.

"The chair recognizes Karl Jenkins," he said, hoping the formality would go at least a little way toward holding tempers in check.

Karl was no politician, but as an ex-Marine he could make a point loudly and clearly, and that was precisely what he intended to do.

"I didn't come here tonight with the idea of being spokesman, but I don't think I'll get any argument when I say that the one thing that everyone in this room wants, the one thing that everyone in this *town* wants, is protection."

A chorus of encouraging shouts filled the room; Karl wisely played it for effect, then raised his hands to quiet the people before Dan could intervene with his gavel.

"Ten people have died in the past two days," he continued, "nine of them citizens of Santa Ynez, and one poor young man who was only passing through. Ten people, slaughtered like cattle! And are we any closer to stopping this maniac than we were this morning, or yesterday?"

The crowd erupted again, and this time Dan didn't wait for Karl to get any extra leverage out of it. He pounded his gavel, calling for immediate order and wishing the six idiot councilmen would do something besides sit there and wonder how all this was going to affect their chances for reelection.

"You're not telling us anything we don't already know, Karl. You think we're proud of what's been happening? The council wants an end to this thing just as much as anyone—or are you forgetting that five of those dead people you were talking about are deputies, and therefore our ultimate responsibility?"

"It's the sheriff's fault. If he knew what he was doing, we'd have had that bastard by now."

"Okay, Karl, give me a for-instance."

"What?"

"If you're so convinced the sheriff's doing such a bad job, it stands to reason you must know what it takes to do a good job. So let's hear it. Give me one or two things guaranteed to catch the guy who's driving that black Car."

Karl felt the crowd grow uneasy around him, and he knew that if he didn't say something soon the edge would shift to Dan.

"We have the right to protect ourselves," he blurted out.

Dan smiled to himself. The door was open for compromise, and Karl had been the first to step through it. Of course he didn't realize that he'd gone exactly where Dan had wanted him to, but then his mind wasn't used to traveling the subtle back roads of politics.

"Just what kind of protection did you have in mind?"

Dan asked, feigning reluctance and dangling the bait like the skilled fisherman that he was.

"A vigilante committee."

Dan leaned to his right and left, conferring with the councilmen, who were more than happy to let him take the lead in this ticklish situation, realizing that the less vocal they were the less they could get blamed for. And if the plan turned out to be a success, they could always claim that they had pledged full support through their silence.

"Well?" Karl prodded, thinking he had the mayor on the defensive. "What's your answer?"

"My answer is that those things can get out of hand pretty easily."

"It seems to me that things are *already* out of hand."

The crowd roared its support, and to the casual observer it looked as if they had the mayor right where they wanted him.

Karl raised his hands for quiet and the noise gradually subsided. An unnatural calm settled over the chamber and the six councilmen shifted uncomfortably in their chairs.

"All right," Dan finally said. "But I'm not going to be forced into authorizing anything illegal."

"Meaning what?"

"Meaning that your citizens can organize for *defensive* purposes only. Anybody with a CB unit can patrol the streets within three blocks of his own house. But I don't want this turning into a heroes' brigade. If anybody sees anything, they're to call the proper authorities. Period."

"By that time he'll be gone," someone shouted from the back.

"And if you start chasing him," Dan said, *"you're*

liable to be the one who's gone. Is anybody here that anxious to be number eleven on the list?"

"All right," Karl said. "We accept your terms."

"Not yet, you don't, because I've got one more condition." The people bristled, knowing what was coming. "Wade Parent remains · sheriff for forty-eight hours."

"And if we say no?"

"I wouldn't recommend it, Karl. You've got a chance at a good compromise. Take it, or you'll force me into decisions none of us will like."

"That's not much of a choice."

"It's the best I can offer. You get your vigilante committee, I get my sheriff, and maybe between us we can prevent another murder. Isn't that really the bottom line? Isn't that why we're all here tonight?"

"We're here to get our town back, to make it safe, and I don't think Wade's the man to do the job."

"You tell me that in two days' time and I'll listen to you. Until then, it's take it or leave it."

"Attitudes like that can make a man awfully unpopular. You ever think about that?"

"You running for mayor, Karl?"

Jenkins blushed with anger. "I'm just trying to get the best deal I can for the town!"

"Well, I just offered it to you, so make up your mind."

"STOP IT! EVERYBODY STOP IT!"

The cry came from the far corner of the room, a hysterical plea that snapped heads around to view the erect, trembling figure of Alice Keil.

"What are you all doing here? What are you all talking about?"

A murmur went through the crowd, the information

spreading quickly that she was the widowed mother of one of The Car's first victims.

"Alice," Dan said soothingly, "why don't you let me have someone drive you to the hospital? You can get a good rest there, and you'll feel much better in the morning."

"I don't need a rest, and I don't need a hospital. All I need is to know what everybody's talking about." Her eyes were unblinking, her vacant stare fixed on a point somewhere above Dan's head.

"We're talking about The Car, Alice. The black Car."

"There's no need to be afraid, you know. It hasn't hurt anybody, not on purpose."

"We got ten dead bodies that say you're wrong, lady. So shut up and sit down!" The angry voice came from a balding, sweaty man in the third row.

"Mister," Dan said with a dangerous calm in his voice, "you make one more remark like that and those boys that drive the ambulance are gonna be busy again."

The man took one look at Dan and slouched sullenly in his chair.

"You're all so frightened," Alice said. "I don't understand it. I don't understand it at all. Suddenly nobody's the way I remember them. The people at the bank all look at me with a strange expression, and this morning a man came for me and took me to see a . . . a dead body. He tried to tell me it was my son, Pete. But of course it wasn't. It wasn't anybody I even knew. Why do you suppose he did that to me? It was cruel, don't you think? Very cruel."

"Please, Alice, you have to accept what's happening. For your own safety."

"NOTHING'S HAPPENING! It's all a pack of lies!

Filthy lies! Why do you want my son to be dead? WHY?"

"We don't, Alice. We don't want *anybody* to be dead. But there's a dangerous man out there. You have to realize that."

"Has anybody seen him?"

"No. Just The Car."

"A black car?"

"That's right," Dan said hopefully.

"But there must be dozens of black cars around. How do you know it's the same one?"

"People have *seen* it, Alice. We have witnesses."

"I don't believe you. Even if somebody *has* been killed, I'm sure it was an accident. People get hit by cars every day. So you see, you're wrong about this thing. Very, very wrong."

"We're wasting time," Karl interrupted. "The quicker we get organized and on the streets, the safer we're all going to be."

"Just remember the ground rules," Dan cautioned.

"Come on," somebody shouted. "Let him do what he wants with his sheriff. We've got work to do."

The crowd shouted its approval and began to empty the room, swirling around Alice Keil, who stood rigid in its midst, flecks of spittle gathering at the corners of her mouth.

Not a single person offered to help her, and soon she was left alone facing the seven men at the large oak table.

Dan leaned over to Sam Cunningham. "Call the hospital and tell them to send an ambulance. I'll take her to my office."

Sam quickly got to his feet, the other five councilmen using his move as an excuse to leave also, anxious to divorce themselves from the issue.

When there were just the two of them, Dan stood up and walked slowly over to Alice. Though her stare was wide-eyed and unwavering, she didn't give the slightest indication that she was aware of his approach.

He touched her arm gently. "Come with me, Alice."

Her only reaction was to raise her hands to her face, then slide them upward into her thick, dark hair.

"Please," Dan said softly, "help is on the way."

Suddenly she clenched her fists and pulled her hands violently away from her head, lacerating her scalp as two tufts of hair came out by the roots.

She looked at the torn hair curiously, trying hard to remember where it came from. Then she sank slowly into a chair, rivulets of blood running down the sides of her face and staining her dress, and Dan could only stand beside her, praying for the sound of the siren and wondering if her snapped mind wasn't more of a salvation than a tragedy.

XXVIII

It was nearly dawn when Wade arrived home. In less than an hour the first light of a new day would pierce the blackness, and he had to be ready. He left his patrol car in the street and walked up the narrow cement path, letting himself in the front door as he'd done so many times in the past. But this wasn't a casual finish to a casual day's work. This was the beginning—and maybe, he thought to himself bitterly, maybe the end.

He threw his jacket on the sofa as he walked through the living room. The house felt somehow alien to him, as if he were a stranger seeing it for the first time, an uninvited guest who had breached its walls for a glimpse of the people who lived inside. He'd been one of them once, but he wasn't any longer. Not with Lauren dead and The Car still alive. He realized that he was thinking about it as a living thing now. He couldn't afford to admit that to anyone else, but he had to admit it to himself. And now that he had, it made things a little easier to take. He didn't feel as impotent as he had when he'd thought he was fighting a simple machine. He laughed at his inverted reasoning, yet it was true. As a man chasing another man in a car, he'd been enraged at his inability to catch it. But as a man chasing a *force*—a cunning, treacherous force—he at least had a temporary excuse for his ineptitude. *Underline the word* temporary, he thought as he stood in the bedroom doorway, looking down at his sleeping children. *Because I have to win. No matter what may be behind that black beast, even if it's Satan himself, I have to win.*

The children stirred and he felt his sadness well up at their mutual loss of Lauren. Once again his daughters had been deprived of the chance to have a complete family, and as growing young girls they would soon need a woman's touch, someone who could give them more than motorcycle rides to school and barbecues on Sundays. Hell, who was he kidding? He had needed her every bit as much as they did, possibly even more. He looked at Margie, asleep in a chair, an open magazine in her lap. *Christ, what they've all got waiting for them when they wake up!* he thought.

He crossed to his own room and stepped inside, staring at the bed he'd shared so often with Lauren. Though he hadn't realized it at the time, things had really been very uncomplicated during those months. And, like most people, when he'd had the moments to savor he hadn't realized how well off he'd been. Right now he'd give anything to be able to look across the room and see her sitting in that damnable lotus position. He'd always thought himself to be a simple, straightforward type of person, but he knew now that she could have taught him volumes about enjoying the real pleasures of life. Why had he been so slow to learn? He found little comfort in the fact that he certainly wasn't alone in his stupidity. What anyone else would have done was beside the point. He'd had his chance and he'd blown it.

He slipped off his shirt and threw it on the bed, emptied his pockets of keys and loose change, and walked

to the closet. He opened the door and stood mesmer-
ized by the facets of his personality that hung before
him: two spare uniforms for work, an inexpensive sport
coat and a couple of ties for those few occasions when
he bothered to dress up, and the pairs of jeans and
casual shirts that he so often threw on without even
realizing what he was wearing. Now that he really
looked at it, he didn't know whether to be proud or
ashamed of his meager wardrobe, but, anyway, it was
him. His life on a few wire hangers. A mindless routine
of work, relaxation, and ventures into other people's
lives.

Until two days ago he'd sailed along like everyone
else in Santa Ynez, calmly indifferent to what was going on around him, the weeks blurring into one another as the spokes of a smoothly revolving wheel
seemed to. . . .

A wheel. The image forced him back to reality and
he reached into the closet, grabbing the clothes he
would need and reminding himself that there was work
to be done.

Dressed for some hard riding, he secured the last
strap on his motorcycle boots. He now faced what he
knew was going to be the most difficult part of his plan
—explaining his action to Debbie and Lynn Marie.

But how? How does a father tell his children that
risking his life is the proper thing to do?

He sat on the bed, trying to crystallize his feelings,
and the more he thought about it, the more untenable
his position became. Revenge? Vindication? Cauteriz-
ing a self-doubt? All those possibilities and more flooded his mind. And while they each may have contained
an element of truth, they were, in the end, ultimately

nothing more than labels, all inadequate at best. He realized then that leaving a note, no matter how sincere, would only raise more questions than it answered. His children had confidence in him, that much he knew. If he were to die, his death would be explanation enough. And if he lived, he'd have the rest of his life to answer their questions.

Enough, then; time to get started.

He crossed to the picture of his father that hung on the wall, removed the badge that was pinned to it, and stuffed it in his shirt pocket. Then, purposely denying himself one final look at his children, he crossed through the house and into the barnlike garage.

His motorcycle was stored in the smaller connecting shed, and he immediately straddled the powerful machine and fired up the engine, wanting to satisfy himself that everything was in absolute working order. He gave the oil time to circulate, then revved the bike to around fifteen-fifty rpm, his ears straining for the slightest hint of anything that was not quite in tune. He caught something, shut off the engine, and walked into the large garage to look for a tool.

The windows admitted the waning light of the moon and the double wooden doors stood closed against the last throes of night. In his impatience, Wade groped among the equipment on the tool bench for what he needed, the dim natural illumination only making things harder. Finally he yanked the cord of an overhead light, but the bare bulb remained unlit. Just as his hand found the familiar contour of the tool he was looking for, he heard a slight movement in the shadows. He froze, gripping the wrench firmly, trying to decide whether he felt the presence of another person. Then a second sound jumped from the stillness—a slight metallic grind, like a gearshift running through a change.

Wade spun around, commanding himself not to believe what he knew would be there. But it was no use, because he was facing it now as it crouched in the shadows, quiet, menacing, semi-visible. The Car.

XXIX

"Lauren? Is that you?"

Margie's sleepy voice shocked Wade out of his paralysis. She stood in the small alcove that connected the house to the garage. *Oh, God,* Wade thought. It was absolutely imperative that she not come any closer.

"Margie, it's Wade. Go back to the children."

"Wade? Where's Lauren? Why aren't you in the hospital?" Her foggy mind could make no sense out of what was happening.

"Never mind that! Just listen to me! You can't come in here; now get back inside."

"What's the matter?" She was more alert now and could hear the fear in his voice.

"Just do as I say!" His eyes never left The Car.

"Wade, for God's sake, tell me what's going on. What's happened to Lauren? Where is she?"

"I'll explain later. Now get *back in the house!* And stay there!"

"All right," she said, trying to pacify him. "I'm going; I'm going."

She backed away into the house and hurried to the telephone. Wade hadn't even looked at her when he'd spoken. Someone was in that garage with him. And what about Lauren? Frantically Margie dialed the number of the sheriff's department. She was halfway through the digits when she realized the line was dead. She stabbed her finger at the disconnect button, let it snap back into place and waited for a dial tone. But nothing came. She pressed the button up and down in rapid succession, hung up the receiver and picked it up again, and still the line refused to work. Then she thought of the children and ran to their bedroom.

They lay safely in bed, sound asleep, and Margie let out an audible sigh. Should she take them and run? But where? No, she told herself, if Wade had said to stay in the house he must have a good reason. Her heart hammering in her chest, she sat down in a chair a few feet from the children's beds and waited, though for what she didn't know.

In the garage, Wade was cornered. He couldn't cross to his motorcycle in the shed because his path would take him directly in front of The Car. He couldn't go into the house because that was almost certain to involve Margie and the children. He let his glance flick to the double doors. They were locked, and a good twelve feet from where he stood.

Slowly, without taking his eyes from The Car, he lowered the wrench that he held, set it on the workbench, and gingerly groped behind him for a large screwdriver, being careful not to jostle any tools against one another. He was just beginning to think it was out of reach when his fingers touched the cold tip of its shaft. Deftly, he inched it across the bench until he held the ribbed handle firmly in his hand. Still The Car made no move, and Wade was grateful for the crisscrossing shadows that offered at least partial concealment.

Once again he measured the distance to the garage doors, and now that he was ready to make his move

they looked to be even farther away than they had before. He started to guess how far he would get before
The Car attacked, but he forced the thought from his
mind. Discipline. Just one step at a time. That's all
he must allow himself to think about. Just one step
at a time. And methodically, like a man inching his
way along a narrow ledge, he moved sideways one
pace to his left.

The Car did nothing.

Wade moved again, covering a little more distance
this time, his eyes boring into the shadows and picking
out the massive lines of the lethal machine, and he
knew that it was scrutinizing him just as carefully.

His legs were working automatically now, bringing
him closer and closer to the double doors. His plan
was a simple one: to lull The Car into his steady
movement and then make a quick break for the doors.
But the execution had to be perfect. In order to give
himself even the ghost of a chance to force the doors
open, he had to take no more than two or three fast
strides to bring himself there. And even then it was
an all-but-impossible gamble.

He was almost halfway there now, his muscles
tensing for the final sprint, when suddenly a muted
glow shone from behind the amber windshield of The
Car. The rapid pace of his own shallow breathing
pounded in Wade's ears, and for one nearly uncontrollable moment he wanted to throw himself on the
long black hood, smash the amber glass and gouge
out the eyes he knew were staring at him. The terrible
eyes he'd seen on Mesa Road.

Now! Wade broke for the garage doors, slamming
into them with his shoulder, jamming the screwdriver
between them and trying to force the hasp out of the

dry, brittle wood. But it wouldn't give, and as he glanced back at The Car he heard its engine come alive with a soft, mocking purr.

He wanted to run, but he made himself hold his position, leaning hard on the screwdriver, forcing himself to use every second the stalking Car was willing to concede. Then it leapt out of the shadows like an angry bull and Wade tore the screwdriver from between the doors, pivoting away toward the workbench, his mind racing to anticipate the next move. But The Car only backed smoothly into its original position and waited.

Again Wade moved to the doors, and again The Car let him grapple with the lock before springing forward and sending him reeling out of the way.

Games! Infuriating games! Wade stood by the workbench, the screwdriver clenched tightly in his fist. Back in position, The Car blipped its accelerator, daring him to make another move. But he held fast, goading the machine into taking the initiative and hoping he could use his maneuverability to put himself behind it and get to his motorcycle in the adjoining shed.

The engine snarled a challenge and still Wade remained motionless. "Come on," he urged. "I'm right here. Come and get me. We're playing by my rules now."

The engine noise increased steadily, exhaust pouring from the tail pipes, carbon monoxide quickly fouling the air. Wade started to cough. He didn't know whether to cover his mouth to protect himself from the fumes or shield his ears from the assaulting noise. Sound waves shook the wooden walls and the exposed rafters and sent a cascade of thick, heavy dust raining down from above.

Wade began to choke, each breath doing him more damage than the last. The awesome power of the engine began to shake the wooden structure as if it were a quivering mold of gelatin; then one of the windows exploded in a shower of flying glass. In the house, the children were awake, clinging to Margie, tears streaming down their faces, trembling in her arms and screaming for their father. But he couldn't hear them; he thought his head was going to come apart from the excruciating agony of The Car's wailing protest. He had to move, to do something, anything, to get out of there, or in a matter of minutes he'd be dead.

He ran for the double doors just as the window between the garage and the shed blew out. His eyes burned from the dust and fumes and his first plunge with the screwdriver missed the crack between the doors; the screwdriver imbedded itself in the wood. He pulled it loose and wedged it home, leaning on it with all his strength. His chest ached for fresh air and he was beginning to feel dizzy. He looked at The Car; it seemed to be swaying back and forth as if it were bobbing on a gentle sea. A vapory blackness was beginning to cloud his thoughts. He pushed harder on the screwdriver, felt something give beneath his weight, and then crashed to the ground, breaking off the handle of the screwdriver, which rolled away across the garage.

Suddenly the engine roar dropped, he heard the gears engage, and The Car sprang forward. He scrambled to his feet and got halfway up, eye-level with the grill and the gaping headlights. For the briefest of intervals he wanted to let go, to give himself up to the crushing impact, but his hold on life was too dear. He felt himself spinning out of the way, his left leg glancing off the smooth chrome of the bumper. Then he flung him-

self across the hood, the touch of the warm metal re-
pulsive to his body, and dove through the shattered
window into the momentary security of the adjoining
shed.

XXX

Wade thudded to the dirt floor, his cracked ribs stabbing him with pain, his head throbbing with the shock of the impact. He pushed himself up on his hands and the world spun violently. *Please,* he whispered to himself, *don't let me pass out.* The spinning slowed; he staggered to his feet and mounted his motorcycle. Reflexes took over as he switched on the ignition and kicked the starter into life. Almost simultaneously there was a splintering crash as The Car smashed through the garage doors, swerving to its left in a frenzied effort to locate its victim.

Wade wheeled his bike through the garage and out the obliterated doors, turning to his right and flicking on his lights to make sure The Car would see him. It immediately skidded into a one-hundred-and-eighty degree turn and hurtled off after the bait.

Though Wade knew his motorcycle was grossly outpowered by the marauding Car, he also knew that his lighter machine could do things his enemy couldn't. That one small advantage and his skill would have to keep him alive long enough to lure the beast to his preplanned destination.

A scant two miles away, a van from the sheriff's department was heading for the same place. Luke was driving. Dalton occupied the other front seat. In the rear were Parker, Thompson, and Fats. Everyone was very quiet, their thoughts locked on two common denominators: their approaching rendezvous with The Car, and the cargo of high explosives that rode with them, lashed to the side panels of the van.

The sky was beginning to brighten with the first wisps of dawn. Deftly, Wade removed the crash helmet that dangled from his handlebars and put it on, the twin headlights of The Car coming up fast in his rearview mirror.

In the hours that he'd been preparing his plan, explaining it in careful detail first to the deputies and then to Amos, he hadn't allowed himself to consider what his feelings would be. But now that events were in motion, he suddenly realized that he was curiously detached from them. Certainly he was aware of all the possibilities, but it was a fatalistic kind of awareness born out of the simple truth that he would either succeed or fail. Perhaps that was what made the whole thing bearable, knowing that there would be no middle ground of doubt to plague him for the rest of his life. Either The Car would be stopped, or it wouldn't. And if he remained alive, he'd have the satisfaction of knowing that this time he'd taken action, this time he hadn't allowed himself to be a pawn of events.

But what if The Car could *never* be stopped? Wade knew that thought should unnerve him, but somehow it didn't. For the first time, he thought of the future as something to be *lived in* rather than something to be manipulated by, and even if that future saw the encroachment of Armageddon, he was ready for it.

The Car was closing the gap steadily now, a black torpedo speeding straight on course. Wade's only hope was that it would toy with him as it had in the past, giving him time to get to the quarry. He snatched the mike from the radio.

"This is Wade! Anybody out there?"

Luke answered the call. "What's your position?"

"Heading east on Twenty-five, about three miles from the quarry, and our boy's right behind me."

"You're too early! We're still on our way, for Christ's sake!"

"What about Amos?" Wade asked anxiously. "Did he get there yet?"

"How the hell do I know? He doesn't have a radio in his truck. Stall, Wade! You've got to get us more time!"

Wade glanced into his rearview mirror. "Shit!"

"What's wrong?" Luke yelled. "What's happening?"

"He just left the road! He's going north across Jilly's Field."

When he heard what was happening, Fats whipped around and looked out the rear window of the van. A fast-approaching dust cloud was visible in the slowly brightening dawn.

"See anything?" Luke asked the deputy.

"Hell, yes! That sonofabitch is coming right behind us!"

Wade's voice cut in over the radio. "Keep heading for the canyon. I'll try to cut across and decoy him."

"He better stand on it," Fats said, " 'cause that mother's coming up fast."

Wade veered off the road and raced his bike across the gray, lifeless landscape, pressing his machine and his skill for all they were worth in a desperate effort to intercept The Car.

The van was on Warm Springs Road, doing a cautious forty-five because of its cargo, the deputies in

the back eyeing the crates of explosives nervously.
Fats kept his vigil at the rear window.

"Push it, Luke! Push it!"

The speedometer edged up to fifty, then fifty-five.
But the grotesque shape of The Car materialized from
the dust cloud and gained on them rapidly.

"He's climbing up our ass!" Fats yelled. "He's
gonna drive right through us!"

Wade saw what was happening, but was still too
far away to be of any help.

The inside of the van was a tableau of impending
disaster. Hal Thompson began to whisper a prayer.
Luke gripped the steering wheel tightly, bracing himself for the impact. But it never came, at least not
when they all expected it, because at the last moment
The Car swerved to its left, pulled up alongside the
van, and bumped it viciously off the road with no more
effort than a horse took to flick its tail at a fly.

The lightweight van careened across the pockmarked
terrain, Luke fighting for control as the deputies were
flung about the cargo area. Parker bruised his left
arm badly against one of the crates. For one frightening instant the van threatened to overturn; then it
settled back to earth with a chassis-wrenching thud.
Larger rocks littered the ground ahead, and Luke was
forced to put the van into a U-turn. The frame
shuddered at the sudden change in direction and the
wooden crates of explosives strained against their lash-
ings.

Then, while the van was still recovering from its
maneuver, The Car came at them again, charging
forward on a broadside collision course. Luke hit the
brakes and twisted the wheel hard to his right, swivel-
ing the van on the front axle. The side of the oncoming
Car scraped viciously along the side of the van. Luke

heard a crash in the cargo area; Dalton looked back just in time to see a boxload of blasting caps spill out across the channeled metal flooring.

The men scrambled for the scattered cargo just as Luke jammed the accelerator to the floor and pulled away from The Car.

"Jesus Christ!" Fats yelled as he slammed into the rear doors. "You're gonna blow us all to hell!"

"Not if that fucking Car does it first!" Luke shot a glance into his rearview mirror and saw something that made him smile. "Looks like our friend ran into a little trouble," he said. The Car's rear wheels were spinning angrily in a natural ravine.

Luke was able to put a hundred yards between his van and the stalled leviathan before it broke free and rocketed forward on another collision course. The deputies continued to gingerly repack the blasting caps, fearing each move would trigger a fatal explosion. The Car halved the distance between them and hurtled on; Luke saw that they were still a good half mile from the canyon and he made a sudden, irrevocable decision. Wheeling the van around behind the jutting corner of a low, gray mesa, he brought the vehicle to a halt.

"Everybody out!" he screamed. "Get the hell out! Jump! He's gonna hit us!"

Without giving them time to think, he cracked his door open, ready to follow his own command. Scant seconds later Dalton had jumped free and the three deputies were piling out through the rear doors, everyone racing up the gentle incline of the mesa, the thundering approach of The Car spurring them to what they prayed would be safety.

Then they heard a familiar sound and knew what was happening. Fats was the first to confirm it when

he looked back over his shoulder and saw the van
spring to life, Luke still at the wheel.

"LUKE! JUMP!"

The others watched in disbelief as the van sped
out into the open, baiting The Car.

"He's staying with it," Thompson said. "He's a
dead man for sure."

Wade crested a nearby mesa and took in the scene
quickly. "Don't do it, Luke," he pleaded into his
mike. "Don't do it, man. Don't do it!"

The Car sped closer and closer, its hulking black
form aching to taste blood.

Gunning his bike into motion, Wade slid down the
sandy soil of the mesa, intersecting with the path of
The Car and daring the charging machine to chase
him. It hesitated for a moment over the choice of
prey, then veered off after Wade—who made sure
to head off in the opposite direction of the retreating
van.

"I've got him, Luke! Pick up your men and get to
the canyon!"

The van wheeled around in a tight U-turn as Wade
replaced his mike and prepared to navigate the rocky
terrain that lay ahead. His only thought was to keep
his bike moving and hope that the black monster
would follow.

Seconds later Luke slid the van to a halt and the
deputies clambered in, feeling the surge of its forward
motion before the doors were even shut.

As they raced for the mouth of the canyon, Luke
felt suddenly embarrassed in the presence of his friends.

"That was a damn fine move," Fats said. "If it
was me, I don't think I could've done it."

Luke smiled. "We don't even know if I could, and
I'm glad we won't have to find out. Now hold on to

those goodies back there so we don't all go up in smoke."

Wade led The Car across the treacherous landscape, his bike an extension of his reflexes and nerve ends. He skirted rocks and leapt potholes, always aware of the snarling menace behind him, but also aware that on terrain like this it was he who had the advantage. And he meant to use it to its fullest. He taunted the lumbering machine, toying with it as it had toyed with so many of its victims, working it into a blind fury, luring it nearer and nearer to the mouth of the box canyon.

Amos Clements' truck sat parked at the top of the canyon (the site of a rock and gravel quarry). Even in the chilly air of the widening dawn his shirt was soaked with sweat from unloading heavy cases of dynamite. The majority of the boxes were already empty, and Chas and Ashberry were planting the final charges at the far side of the narrow canyon. They worked quickly and surely, having learned fast under Amos' harsh but professional direction. He'd proven to be a tireless worker himself, and they were thankful to have his expertise on their side.

"Think this'll work?" Ashberry asked, leaning on his shovel. He was digging the shallow holes, Chas positioning the charges and pushing some dirt back in to hold them in place. After their initial mistakes they'd soon found a rhythm to their task and had progressed very rapidly.

Chas looked up at his partner. "If Wade's still alive, it'll work."

"And you think he is?"

"If you're asking does he have a chance, my answer's yes. If you're asking is it a good one, who knows?

All I can tell you is *I* sure wouldn't want to be riding around out there with that thing breathing down my neck."

Suddenly Chas stood up, listening hard for something. Ashberry started to speak, but Chas cut him off with a quick motion of his hand. Then the other deputy heard it—a muted rumble in the distance—and his apprehension quickly settled into a heavy lump of fear.

"There're two of 'em," Chas said. "One's a bike. And they're coming our way. Fast."

"Christ, the other truck isn't even here yet."

The throb of the engines was louder now, and Amos looked up from his truck, where he was shouldering two spindles of electric wire he'd just unloaded.

"Now haul ass!" he yelled across the canyon. "Or it's all over!"

Chas and Ashberry rushed to plant their final sticks of dynamite while Amos dropped the spindles of wire, grabbed a heavy knotted rope from the bed of the truck, and ran to a large rock at the edge of the box end of the canyon. He tossed one end of the rope over, securing the other to the rock, all the while watching the steady progress of Wade and The Car toward the mouth of the canyon. The single headlight of the motorcycle was bouncing across the landscape like a frightened rabbit.

"God help him," Amos murmured, and he gave a solid tug on the knot binding the rope to the rock.

"Damnit, we're going to be too late!" Luke jockeyed the van along the rim of the canyon, only a few yards from the top.

Below, Wade raced through the mouth, heading straight for the wall of rock and earth that lay a quarter of a mile ahead. The Car charged after him, the reverberations of its angry roar bouncing off the cliffs on either side.

Luke's van skidded to a stop near Amos' truck and the men piled out.

"No time to position your stuff!" Amos was carrying the spindles of wire. "Just put as many crates as you can along there!" He pointed to the base of a hill that stood near a footbridge connecting the two sides of the canyon. The deputies set quickly to work while Amos continued to play out the wire to the preset blasting caps and charges.

On the floor of the canyon, Wade reached the cul-de-sac and wrenched his bike in a tight circle, bringing it to a stop. Behind him and to either side stood hundred-foot cliffs of rock. He had no way of knowing how many explosives his men had been able to lay down. His head was pounding from his efforts and his vision was slipping in and out of focus. The adrenaline was coursing through his body and he had fleeting thoughts of Lauren, his children, and whether or not he was strong enough to do what was expected of him, what he expected of himself. But he couldn't worry about that now, because directly in front of him was The Car. Engine roaring. Tires spitting loose gravel. Hurtling toward him like a runaway locomotive, ready to snuff out his life.

XXXI

Timing was everything. Wade held his position until the last possible moment, then shot to his right, out of the path of the oncoming Car, and circled around behind it.

Enraged at its missed opportunity, The Car spun for another attack, springing forward in a surge of momentum, small stones clattering off its undercarriage in a tarantella of furious motion. Wade gunned his bike and raced along parallel to the east wall of the canyon, heading back toward the mouth. Then his front wheel caught a particularly soft patch of earth and his machine was suddenly careening out of control. He tried to steady the tipping bike with his foot; his shoulder slammed into the rock wall and his vision blurred terribly. His fading senses told him he had to move or die, and somehow he managed to recover his balance and pull away just as The Car scraped along the wall behind him, the grating sound of metal against rock combining with the relentless throb of the engine to create a thundering, blood-lusting cry.

Wade felt the strength oozing from his body. His head was a whirling mass of pain and he knew he could play matador to the killer bull no longer. He spun his bike around and headed for the cul-de-sac, hoping he could reach the rope before The Car overtook him.

It required every ounce of skill and will power he possessed to keep his machine steady beneath him. A ten-foot pile of gravel stood just to the left of the dangling rope. Or was it to the right? Or directly in front of it? His optic nerves were shifting the scenery back and forth, badgering him with cruel illusions, hiding reality like the pea in a shell game.

The Car closed in from behind, the hot breath of its engine beating against his back. He had a brief vision of being scooped up between the bulbous headlights and flung into the air, when suddenly he was looking up at the brightening sky, his bike churning up the gravel pile that he had reached long before his eyes told him he should have.

It wasn't until the motorcycle started falling back against him that his impaired reflexes forced him to bail out, the bike flipping over backward and smashing down onto the hood of The Car.

Wade felt the impact of his body against the earth, was certain he would pass out, and then found himself running toward the rope that hung down the back wall of the canyon. Behind him, The Car was swerving madly, trying to shake the heavy bike off its hood. Wade lunged for the rope and came up with a handful of air. He swept his arm wildly through the phantom images until he felt the slap of the fibers against his skin. And with all his strength he grabbed hold and began to climb.

His feet dug into the canyon wall as he grappled hand-over-hand for the support of the knots. Then he felt the earth shudder violently around him as The Car smashed into the wall. There was a sickening crumble and a large part of the vertical rock projection slid away from beneath Wade's feet, leaving him swaying in the air above the incensed predator.

The Car backed off for another assault. Wade let go
with his left hand and reached up for the next knot,
but without the support of the wall beneath his feet it
was a terrific strain and his hand fell short just as The
Car slammed again into the canyon wall. For a terrible
moment he hung by one hand, then swung his left up
again and this time caught the knot. The Car backed
away; the earth began to crack above Wade, but still he
reached up with his right hand and hoisted his body a
little higher with an agonizing effort. His legs flailed in
the air, searching desperately for a foothold; his muscles began to quiver and he knew it wouldn't be long
before they turned to pulp and let him fall.

"Hold on! We'll pull you up!"

The voice barely penetrated his scrambled senses,
then he felt a tug on the rope and lifted his head to see
Luke and Dalton at the rim of the canyon. He wondered how many of the others had made it when he
heard Amos Clements shouting something about wires.
That would mean the explosives were in place. *We've
got a chance*, he told himself. *Jesus, we've got a chance.*

There was another crash as The Car rammed the
wall again, and Wade felt the rope shift suddenly as it
slipped into a tight, jagged crevice.

"It's jammed!" Luke yelled. "Climb, Wade! Climb!"

With a supreme effort of will he banished the pain
and weakness and reached up with his left hand for the
next knot. As soon as he felt its support he followed
with his right, knowing that once he stopped he'd never
have the power to begin again.

"Just one more," Dalton urged. "Then we can reach
you." The two deputies lay on their stomachs, their
arms extending over the edge, waiting to grab hold of
Wade.

His left hand strained for the knot and Luke immediately clamped onto Wade's wrist. In another few seconds Dalton had his other arm. Wade's feet finally found some leverage and he was able to ease the load on the deputies. Then they struggled to their knees and dragged him over the top.

It was only then that he realized it had been too long since the tremor of The Car's last attack. The three of them looked down into the canyon and saw the black beast approaching the mouth and the open terrain beyond.

"Shit!" Dalton said. "He's leaving."

But when The Car reached the entrance to the canyon it veered sharply to its right and onto the road that would carry it up to the rim.

Wade took in the flurry of activity as Amos and the others completed the final stages of wiring the charges.

Luke was about to yell a warning when Amos looked across and saw for himself what was happening. He turned to Ashberry, who was standing with him on the bridge.

"Bring the detonator!" Amos ordered. "Fast!"

Ashberry raced for the detonator, pulled it from Amos' truck, and set it down behind a large rock pile while Amos played out two spindles of wire back toward the critical piece of equipment.

The Car thundered in the background as Chas rushed over to Amos and relieved him of one of the heavy spindles. The two men broke into a run, moving toward the detonator.

Luke and Dalton helped Wade to his feet just as The Car began to sound staccato blasts of victory on its horn.

"I'm okay," Wade lied. "Now run! Save yourselves!"

Dalton hesitated, then ran off, afraid to look behind him when he didn't hear any following footsteps.

Wade stumbled off in the opposite direction, toward a low-lying hill that skirted a portion of the canyon rim. The same hill where Luke's men had planted their cases of explosives.

"This way!" Luke screamed. "He'll see you up there!"

Wade pushed himself into an agonizing sprint and was halfway up the hill before Luke grabbed one of his legs and tried to pull him down, but Wade twisted free and crested the incline.

Chas and Amos pounded to the detonator, falling to their knees when they reached it and immediately going about the task of cutting the wires and skinning back the raw ends.

The Car cannoned into view at the rim of the canyon as Luke scrambled up the hill to Wade. They were both in plain view of the crazed beast and it altered its course, heading straight for them.

"Come on!" Luke cried frantically. "You're crazy! He'll kill us if we don't get out of here!"

The Car screamed forward, its horn still blaring, its grotesque black form smelling death. In another instant it was angling up the hill, its canted fenders and vertical grill only a few feet from the two men.

"Now!" Wade commanded, and they dove apart, rolling down the far side of the hill.

The Car braked immediately to intercept its dodging prey, but its momentum was too great and it skidded across the top of the hill and down the other side, the length of its sleek, vicious body gliding past Wade, missing him by only inches. He saw that its wheels were locked in a mighty effort to keep its hurtling mass from reaching the rim of the canyon.

Luke was running for cover, Wade scrambled to his feet and whirled in the direction of the detonator.

"HIT IT!" His legs pushed him forward. "HIT THE DAMNED THING!"

As Amos jammed the raw edges of the wires into contact, Chas pushed down hard on the plunger.

The rim of the canyon disintegrated beneath The Car and the behemoth slid into space, the explosion almost eclipsed by an unearthly, nerve-shattering bellow as the beast plunged downward.

The shock waves lifted Wade and Luke off their feet and dashed them to the ground. Then a towering column of orange flame spewed up from the quarry, scorching the innocent dawn with its savage fury. As the men watched in wide-eyed horror the flame sculpted itself into a glowing claw of vengeance that threatened to reach down from the sky and snatch them away. An instant later it appeared as a horrible, twisted face—a gargoyle etched in tongues of flame.

Then it was gone, and the stifling quiet of morning settled over the scene.

Slowly, the motionless figures began to stir, first one and then another rising to his feet and brushing the dust from his clothes with a dazed sense of anticlimax.

Wade and Luke moved to the demolished rim of the canyon and looked down to its floor, which was littered with the debris of the explosion.

Wade heard himself speak the long-awaited epitaph.

"Whoever he was, he isn't any more. It's all over."

"Didn't you see it?" Luke asked hollowly. "In the fire?"

"It's buried under a hundred tons of rock."

"No."

The sound floated down from the surrounding mountains, cutting off Wade's reply. Then it came again and the others turned around, stunned by the realization of what they were hearing, assaulted by the faint but unmistakable sound of a car's revving engine.

It quickly grew in intensity, ricocheting off the majestic peaks, soon joined by the triumphant blast of a horn. The Car's horn. Then others entered the demonic symphony, horns of different pitch and character, all building in a strident crescendo of dark prophecy.

Wade walked away from the canyon. He wanted to go home. He wanted to get his children and live whatever time was left.

"FAR BETTER THAN *JAWS!*"
—*Kirkus Reviews*

The Dogs

by Robert Calder

The Alpha Litter are an experimental breed of canines. Keenly intelligent, of sensory superiority. Alertness and stress tolerance exceptional. Strong and assertive . . . capable of massive, vicious aggression.

At the age of 15 weeks one male is missing.

And a hundred miles away Alex Bauer has found a puppy. Soon, in a quiet New England town, man has lost control, and the beasts are loose.

"Startlingly ferocious and terrifyingly effective . . . gripping all the way to the final hunt." —*Library Journal*.

A DELL BOOK $1.95 (2102-29)

Dell Bestsellers

- ☐ **THE HITE REPORT** by Shere Hite $2.75 (13690-3)
- ☐ **THE BOYS FROM BRAZIL** by Ira Levin $2.25 (10760-1)
- ☐ **THE GEMINI CONTENDERS**
  by Robert Ludlum $2.25 (12859-5)
- ☐ **MARATHON MAN** by William Goldman $1.95 (15502-9)
- ☐ **THE RHINEMANN EXCHANGE**
  by Robert Ludlum $1.95 (15079-5)
- ☐ **RICH FRIENDS** by Jacqueline Briskin $1.95 (17380-9)
- ☐ **SEVENTH AVENUE** by Norman Bogner $1.95 (17810-X)
- ☐ **THRILL** by Barbara Petty $1.95 (15295-X)
- ☐ **THE TURNCOAT** by Jack Lynn $1.95 (18590-4)
- ☐ **FOR US THE LIVING**
  by Antonia Van Loon $1.95 (12673-8)
- ☐ **THE NINTH MAN** by John Lee $1.95 (16425-7)
- ☐ **THE DOGS** by Robert Calder $1.95 (12102-7)
- ☐ **NAKOA'S WOMAN** by Gayle Rogers $1.95 (17568-2)
- ☐ **ALLIGATOR** by Shelley Katz $1.95 (10167-0)
- ☐ **THE CHOIRBOYS** by Joseph Wambaugh $2.25 (11188-9)
- ☐ **NIGHTWORK** by Irwin Shaw $1.95 (16460-5)
- ☐ **SHOGUN** by James Clavell $2.75 (17800-2)
- ☐ **WHERE ARE THE CHILDREN?**
  by Mary H. Clark $1.95 (19593-4)